# KEVIN MARKEY

**HARPER**
*An Imprint of* HarperCollins*Publishers*

Library of Congress Cataloging-in-Publication Data
Markey, Kevin.
　Rainmaker / by Kevin Markey. — 1st ed.
　　p. cm. — (The super sluggers)
　Summary: The Rambletown Rounders want to end
their last season together with a fun-filled rafting trip
and a championship win, but star pitcher Slingshot
Slocum hits a slump, believing the drenching rains
that threaten to ruin their adventure are his fault.
　ISBN 978-0-06-115228-3 (trade bdg.)
　[1. Baseball—Fiction. 2. Rain and rainfall—Fiction.
3. Self-confidence—Fiction.] I. Title.
PZ7.M3394546Rai 2012　　　　　　　　2011019365
[Fic]—dc23　　　　　　　　　　　　　　　　CIP
　　　　　　　　　　　　　　　　　　　　　　AC

Typography by Larissa Lawrynenko
12　13　14　15　16　　LP/RRDH　　10　9　8　7　6　5　4　3　2　1
❖
First Edition

For N & S, as always

# ★ CHAPTER 1 ★

"Uh-oh," I said.

I could have been talking about the weather. The on-again, off-again rain that had been spitting down all afternoon was starting again.

But I wasn't. I was talking about our pitcher, Slingshot Slocum. He was struggling.

The Rambletown ace kicked high and fired his seventeenth pitch of the fifth inning.

The Lumleyville Lumberjack hitter grinned as the ball sailed wide, slapping into Tugboat Tooley's big pie plate of a catcher's mitt a good foot outside the strike zone. It might as well have missed by a mile.

"BALL FOUR!" barked the umpire. "TAKE YOUR BASE!"

The batter didn't need an invitation. He was already trotting up the line, the third straight Lumleyville hitter to draw a walk.

Normally Slingshot is lights out. Now he had loaded the bases in a playoff game. With nobody out, and leading by only a run, we were in a jam.

Against the lowly Lumberjacks, no less.

Don't get me wrong. I have nothing against the Lumberjacks. They're a good bunch of guys. Friendly, cheerful, never spit on their palms for the postgame hand slap. They just happen to stink at baseball.

Year after year, Lumleyville fields one of the worst teams in the ten-to-twelve division. Put it this way: The Lumberjacks are much better at chopping lumber than at swinging it. It was shocking that they had even made the playoffs. Meanwhile, we're pretty good. Usually.

After all, we're the defending champs.

At the moment, we looked more like chumps than champs. Another walk and the Lumberjacks would tie the score. A hit would blow the game wide open. A loss would end our season.

The thought of bowing out in the first round of the playoffs was horrible. From opening day, way back in Rambletown's freakishly frigid spring, our team goal had been to make it to the title game. We had worked our tails off all summer, knowing we would never get another chance to play for the championship. This was our last year together as a team. Next season, a bunch of us would be moving up to a new age bracket. None of us knew which of a dozen different teams we might wind up on. Only one thing was certain: Soon the Rambletown Rounders as we loved them would be finished. More than anything, we wanted to go out with a bang. We wanted to win one last title.

If we somehow survived the playoffs, we fully expected to face the Hog City Haymakers in the championship game. When it came to winning pennants, our archrivals were like the Pizza Palace of baseball. They delivered. The Haymakers have a pitcher named Flicker Pringle who leads the league in wins, strikeouts, and earned run average. Not to mention brushback pitches, high cheese, and chin music. In other words, he's not afraid to go after batters. Flicker believes home plate belongs to him alone. The rest of us approach it at our own peril.

On top of being scary good, Flicker Pringle and the Haymakers are big. Big and mean and hairy. Half the guys on that team have beards. Pretty strange for a bunch of eleven-year-olds. The other half look like they spend their free time messing around with pianos. Lifting them, not playing them.

As surely as the distance from home to first is sixty feet, the road to the pennant ran through the Haymakers. But first we had to take care of the Lumberjacks.

"Settle down now, kid!" I called from my position at third base as Tugboat gunned the

4

ball back to Slingshot.

Our pitcher snapped the ball out of the mist with a look of disgust. He mopped his face with his sleeve. He stared home for the sign. Tugboat flashed one finger: fastball. Slingshot shook him off. Tugboat gave him the sign for changeup. Slingshot shook him off again.

I groaned. I hoped Slingshot wasn't thinking about throwing the forkball. For some reason known only to himself, lately Slingshot had been obsessed with mastering the forkball, a kind of pitch that dives away from batters before reaching the plate. It's called a forkball because of the grip: You spread your index and middle fingers wide and fork the ball between them. The problem is, the forkball is a terrible pitch if you're a kid. You have to snap your wrist hard to make the ball spin, and the strain can really mess up your arm. No one younger than seventeen or eighteen should fool with it. Everybody knows that. And yet Slingshot kept trying.

The other problem with the forkball was

accuracy. Slingshot's version of it was like a bacon double cheeseburger at a vegetarian restaurant. It never crossed the plate.

"Nothing fancy!" I called. "Just hum it in there!"

Slingshot brought his hands together over his head.

That's when the rain really began to fall.

Only "fall" is not the right word for what the rain did. It crashed upon Rambletown Field like a tidal wave, a sudden, drenching wall of water. And it kept right on pounding.

Mayhem erupted in the bleachers as fans scrambled to escape the deluge. As wet as it was, they could've used scuba gear. We could have, too. Or maybe a submarine. Within seconds, the field flooded. So much water fell so fast that the bases rose and began drifting around the swamped diamond, Lumleyville runners clinging to them like Titanic survivors.

"The runners are going!" I shouted as water swirled up to my ankles. Between the hammering rain and all the thunder, no one heard me.

Fortunately, it didn't matter. As I shouted, the umpire jumped from behind the plate. He raised his arms and called off the game.

At least I think he did. It was hard to tell. The solid rush of water from the sky blurred everything like a shower curtain. For all I know, the ump might have been casting a net into the rolling sea.

In any case, I didn't wait for a second opinion. I waded off the field and into the shelter of the dugout, where Mr. Bones greeted me with a wet smack on the chops.

Mr. Bones is my dog, a long-nosed, short-legged, yellow-haired fur ball that strangers often mistake for a bandicoot. He likes to be petted, and he likes to lick faces. Judging by the way he danced and yapped on the top step of the dugout as my fellow Rounders splashed in from the storm, he does not like thunder and lightning.

Or rainouts.

Or baseball fields when they turn into the Atlantic Ocean.

One after another, the guys streamed down the concrete steps like rats abandoning a sinking ship. A real ship would have been nice. We could have used it to sail to higher ground.

Shortstop Stump Plumwhiff whipped off his cap and wrung it out like a dishrag. It was a shocking sight. Stump never takes off his cap. He wears it to school, to camp, to bed. I know this for a fact, because we've been best friends forever and we often have sleepovers.

"Some storm." He whistled, squashing the waterlogged cap back atop his red hair, which, for the first time in all the years I'd known him, wasn't standing up. It was plastered to his head like it'd been painted on with a floor mop.

"Cats and dogs," I agreed.

Mr. Bones let out a yelp.

"Sorry, pal," I said. "Just an expression."

"More like elephants and hippos," offered

Ocho James, our crackerjack right fielder. "It's heavy, man!"

We gazed out across the diamond. The last Lumleyville base runner was using second base like a boogie board, thrashing his way through the surf toward the visitors' dugout. Forming a human chain, his teammates reached out and reeled him home.

In our own dugout, Skipper Skip-to-My-Lou Clementine thought it wise to undertake a head count. Standard practice in a natural disaster, I guess.

"Tugboat Tooley?" Skip called.

"Here," said our catcher.

"Gilly and Billy Wishes?"

"Here and here, Skip," chimed the brothers. Gilly plays first; his kid brother, Billy, helps out as batboy. He'll be a great player himself in a few years, when he's old enough to join a team. In the meantime, we love having him around as batboy. For one thing, he's just a good kid. For another, he's luckier than the number seven. I always rub his head before going up to bat.

"Glove Rodriguez."

"Here," replied our second baseman.

"Stump Plumwhiff."

"Present and accounted for."

"Walloper?"

"Right over here, Skip," I said.

Walloper is my nickname. It's short for the Great Walloper, on account of I like to wallop the tar out of the ball. Ever since the peewees, hitting home runs has come naturally to me. My real name is Banjo H. Bishbash. Fortunately, nobody except my parents and teachers use it. Long story. Banjo was my grandfather's name. According to family lore, he was born with a big round head on a skinny lollipop stick of a body. His folks took one look and called him Banjo. My dad got the name next. Then he gave it to me. Suffice it to say, my family has a strong sense of tradition and an even more powerful sense of humor. I do, too. With a name like Banjo, what choice do I have?

"Ocho James?"

"High and dry," announced the right fielder.

"Gasser Phipps?" called Skip.

"Present," replied Gasser, who patrols center field when weather allows.

"Ducks Bunion?"

"Yes," said Ducks, who despite his nickname is no fonder of rain than the rest of us. They say he waddled when he was learning to walk as a little kid.

"Velcro Ramirez?"

"Here." Velcro moved to Rambletown from Florida last year. He's probably more used to tropical monsoons than the rest of us.

"Slingshot Slocum?"

No answer.

"Slingshot?" Skip Lou called again, glancing up from his clipboard.

Still no answer.

He wasn't in the dugout. I swiveled my head around and peered through the murk of the field. That's when I spotted him.

Our pitcher stood atop the mound, the very crown of which was still above water. Just barely. Waves lapped at the rubber. Head down, shoulders hunched, Slingshot looked like a shipwrecked sailor marooned on a tiny, quickly disappearing island.

"Slingshot," I yelled. "Get in here!"

Maybe he didn't hear me over the pounding rain. Maybe he was ignoring me on purpose. In any case, he didn't look up. He just kept slamming a sopping-wet ball into his sodden mitt.

Clearly, giving up all those walks was messing with his head. But this was no time to worry about pitching. If we didn't get out of there in a hurry, we'd need to swim for it. Already rainwater was cascading down the steps and filling the dugout.

"Go!" ordered Skip Lou. "You guys get home. We've got Bixburg tomorrow if the weather improves."

"We can't just leave him," I protested.

"You're right," said Skip Lou. "We can't.

He'll be swept out to sea."

Skip zipped his windbreaker up to his chin and dashed to the mound. Stump and I splashed after him. Mr. Bones doggie paddled behind us.

Slingshot did not greet us with open arms. In fact, he crossed them over his chest and glowered at us.

"Leave me in, Skip," he pleaded. "I'll get the next guy out. I know I will."

"The game's over, Slingshot," Skip said. "C'mon, let's go." He held out his hand for the ball.

"It's not over," Slingshot insisted. "I'm telling you, I feel fine."

"Glad to hear it, son," Skip said gently. "But the game really is over. For all of us."

"It's raining," Stump pointed out. "Pretty hard. In case you hadn't noticed."

"Rain?" Slingshot asked. He held out his hand, palm up. His eyes were blank. He wasn't kidding.

Skip and Stump and I exchanged glances.

This did not look good. Not good at all.

A wicked crack of thunder shook the park. The rain hammered down like nails.

"I can beat those guys," Slingshot muttered. "I know I can!"

We hustled him off the field.

# ★ CHAPTER 2 ★

Slingshot, Stump, Mr. Bones, and I made a beeline for the bike rack at the edge of the parking lot.

We always rode to home games. It was a tradition. In baseball you don't mess with tradition. Only bad things can happen if you do. Of course, bad things can happen even if you don't.

Things like your pitcher going bonkers in the middle of a tight game. And Lumleyville loading the bases on walks.

And monsoons.

I just hoped our bikes hadn't been swept away by now.

Mr. Bones beat us to the rack. Our bikes were still where we'd locked them. I unchained my silver twelve-speed and wheeled it to the edge of a giant puddle.

"We'll never get across without pontoons," I said. "There's no way we can ride in this."

My friends pulled up next to me. The rain continued to lash down.

"What have we got to lose?" said Stump. "It's not like we can get any wetter."

Mr. Bones took that as his cue to charge into the puddle. His short legs disappeared. Then his long middle went under. When only the tips of his ears showed above the ripples, I started to get nervous.

"Mr. Bones," I shouted. "Swim for it!"

An instant later, he emerged on the other side: ears first, then nose, shoulders, tail, and legs. He looked like a different dog when he came up out of the morass. Much smaller. He gave a tremendous shake, shedding gallons of water from his fur, and puffed back up almost to his normal size, which is not huge to begin with. He's what you'd call a low-slung dog.

Just then a car plowed across the parking lot, lights flashing and horn beeping. I recognized my mom's minivan at once. Water reached halfway up the tires. Normally we pedal home from games. It's a tradition, and you know how I feel about those. Today I was happy for the lift. Things were already so weird I didn't think one more change could hurt.

My dad hopped out of the passenger seat and helped us load our bikes in the back.

"Wow," he said once we were safely inside. "Some storm."

"Buckle up, everyone," Mom called from behind the wheel. "This could get interesting."

She tapped the gas, and we sluiced forward like a ferryboat pulling away from a dock.

"Bang bang, chitty chitty, bang bang," Dad sang.

I groaned. Dad may not be the world's worst singer, but no one is ever going to confuse him with Luciano Pavarotti either. What he lacks in talent, he makes up for in sheer volume. You ever hear a bull moose bellowing in pain? I haven't either. But I imagine it would sound something like my dad singing. I mean he is *loud*. I started to roll down my window but quickly thought better of it. As hard as the rain was falling, the van would have flooded in a heartbeat.

"In the movie, doesn't the car fly and float?" I shouted.

A pair of wings would have been nice. We could've used them to take off to someplace where baseball games never get washed out. The Mojave Desert sounded promising.

Mom flipped on the radio. Instantly the smooth voice of Louie "the Lip" Leibenstraub filled the van, mercifully drowning out Dad's singing.

"It's wet out there," crooned the DJ. "So keep your umbrellas handy and keep your radios tuned to WHOT, Hot 102.5, for the best music and the latest weather reports. Now, in honor of the freak gullywasher that has settled over Rambletown, here's a blast from the past by Mr. Burt Bacharach. Feel free to sing along."

"Please do not," I groaned, "feel free to sing along."

Too late. Dad had already launched into a corny song about raindrops and how they kept falling on his head.

By the time the van floated into the driveway fifteen minutes later, I would have gladly traded a week of sunshine for some peace and quiet. But at least the storm seemed to be tapering off. The rain gushed down with only slightly more force than a fire hose. Slingshot was showing signs of improvement, too. The dazed look was gone from his face, and he seemed to know where he was.

We bumped open the doors and raced into the house, where Mr. Bones nearly gave my mom a heart attack by shaking himself like a bottle of salad dressing. Water sprayed all over the kitchen.

"Mr. Bones, no!" Mom shouted. "Why does

he always do that in the house?"

"What would be the point of doing it out in the rain?" Dad laughed. "He'd never get dry."

"Quiet, you!" Mom growled. She rushed off to find towels.

Dad chuckled. "How about you guys go change into dry clothes? I'll call Slingshot's and Stump's parents to let them know they're here. Then we can see about some lunch."

Lunch sounded good. I was starving.

We kicked off our cleats by the door and slopped up to my room. My mom passed us on the stairs, carrying an armload of towels. She tossed a couple to us, took one look at the trail of water in our wake, and went back for more.

In my room, I dug through the closet for some clothes that I thought would fit my friends.

"Try these," I said tossing a random mix of shirts, jeans, and sweatpants on the bed.

"So, Slingshot," Stump asked as he pulled a green-and-gold Oakland A's throwback jersey over his head. "What happened out there today?" He checked himself in the mirror on the back of the door. "Sweet."

"What do you mean?" Slingshot asked. My old gray sweatpants came about halfway down his calves. They looked like knickers on him.

"Three straight walks on twelve balls in a row is what I mean." Stump had never been shy about getting right to the point. "Slick outfit, by the way. Where are the animals?"

"Huh?" Slingshot asked.

"You look like Noah, dude. Those sweats are floods."

"We could've used an ark," I said.

"We could've used a strike," Stump said.

"Look, I'm sorry, okay?" Slingshot choked. His face glowed as red as a birthday balloon. The thing about balloons, they always pop. Slingshot looked like he might burst, too. "I don't know what happened," he continued. "My control just . . . I don't know. I couldn't find the zone."

"The ball was slippery," I said. "Anyway, we

were leading in the fifth when the game was called, so it's a win. We're still alive."

"No, Stump's right," Slingshot said. "I stunk. It's the worst I've ever pitched in my life."

"You should lay off the stupid forkball," Stump said. "You're going to wreck your arm. Besides, you can't even get it over the plate."

"I get it over in practice all the time."

"Well, you shouldn't," Stump chided. "It's going to mess you up! Plus, you don't need it. Your other stuff is great." He ran a towel over his hair. It sprang up to its normal height, and he slapped his baseball cap over it.

"Not today, it wasn't," Slingshot croaked, sounding like a frog. A real frog would have been nice. Frogs are amphibious. We could have learned a thing or two from them about hopping around swamped bases like they were lily pads. "The drizzle wasn't the problem. The ball felt fine coming out of my hand. I just couldn't put it where I wanted."

A horrible thought crossed my mind when

he said that. Earlier in the season, Stump had been laid low by a nasty case of the yips. His throwing accuracy had completely deserted him. The harder he tried, the worse he played. It was painful to watch, the way he sprayed balls all over the infield. I hoped something similar wasn't happening to Slingshot.

Before I could mention this gruesome idea—not that I was sure I even wanted to—my dad interrupted our conversation. "Lunch is on, guys," he called from the foot of the stairs. "Come and get it!"

The smell of fried baloney wafted up with his words. Fried baloney sandwiches are my favorite. My mouth started to water.

The sandwiches must have smelled just as good to Mr. Bones. He shot off the bed like a lighting bolt. We raced after him. We knew if we didn't, there would be nothing left for us to eat.

# ★ CHAPTER 3 ★

**D**ad had been busy.

A small mountain of sandwiches waited for us on the table. I hadn't seen so much baloney in one place since the movie *Transmutants II: Revenge of the Mudmen* played at the mall.

"Don't be shy, boys!" Dad called from the stove. "Plenty more coming." He wielded a black spatula and wore a goofy apron embroidered in pink with the image of a laughing pig.

I don't know where he gets those things. Or why Mom lets him keep them.

Slingshot, Stump, and I pulled up chairs. Outside the kitchen window, the trees dripped and puddles pocked the lawn like stepping-stones, but the rain had nearly stopped.

We started munching.

The thing about fried baloney sandwiches is, they cure bad moods. Whenever I feel really down about something, I eat a pile of them. Like a hitting slump, say, or a stupid argument, or when your ace pitcher, who happens to be one of your two best friends on earth, suddenly loses his mojo smack in the middle of a pennant race. Little stuff like that.

Something about fried baloney makes you feel better. Maybe it's just the name. You got to admit, baloney is kind of a funny word. Try saying it and frowning at the same time. You can't.

Normally I sizzle up the sandwiches myself. Then I split them with Mr. Bones. A fried baloney sandwich for me, a fried baloney sandwich for him. On a really bad day, like the one when I whiffed four times in a single game, we'll go through a pound of baloney and a whole loaf of Old Leadbelly Sinker bread.

Today I was more than happy to let Dad do

the cooking and to share lunch with Stump and Slingshot. If anyone needed his spirits raised, it was Slingshot.

"What in the world are you mumbling about?" Stump suddenly asked.

I looked up. He and Slingshot stared across the table at me.

"What?" I asked. At least I meant to. With my mouth full, it came out more like *"Whmmph."* I swallowed hard and tried again. "I didn't say anything."

"Did too," said Slingshot.

"Sounded like 'Baloney, baloney, baloney.'"

"Did I actually say that out loud?" I blushed. "I was just thinking about what a weird word it is."

"You know what's weird?" Stump asked.

"What?"

"You!"

He and Slingshot cracked up. Then they both reached for sandwiches. It was good to see Slingshot smiling again. I snagged another sandwich for myself.

I was about to take a bite when, suddenly, an earthquake struck. Or at least that's what it felt like. I looked down and saw Mr. Bones parked beside my chair, his tail wagging so hard that the whole table shook.

"Sorry, buddy," I said. I fed him a sandwich. He wagged even harder. At least seven point zero on the Richter scale.

Mom hurried into the kitchen.

"What on earth is all that noise?" she asked, coughing from baloney smoke.

"Lunch," I said.

She looked at us stuffing our faces with fried baloney sandwiches. She looked at Mr. Bones chomping and wagging under the table.

"I think I'll make a salad," she said.

We finished eating without any more seismic shocks. After clearing our plates, we tried to figure out what to do with the rest of the afternoon. Even though the rain had now stopped, the ground was still way too wet to play outside.

"Wii Sports?" Stump asked.

"Watch a movie?" said Slingshot.

"I'm game for anything," I said.

"Pick up the playroom?" suggested Mom.

"Anything except that," I groaned.

"What we should do," said Dad, "while you guys are all here, is go over plans for our rafting trip one last time."

"Great idea!" I agreed, relieved to be off the hook for the playroom.

In just a few days, the whole team was supposed to set off down the Big Fork River. We'd been planning the trip ever since spring, when the baseball schedule came out and we saw that there was a three-day break between the end of the playoffs and the championship game. All season long, our goal had been to make it to that game. Now a chance at the championship no longer looked like a sure thing. But the trip definitely was going to happen. Not even bad pitching could keep us from *that*.

The idea was to load the cars and drive up to

North Woods Park, where dads and kids would spend a couple days paddling the river, camping for a night along the way.

Moms had been invited, too, but for some reason none of them had been all that enthusiastic about coming along. I think what bothered them was bug juice. That's what our dads always called Kool-Aid whenever the subject of food and drink came up. I don't know why they called it that. You've got to admit, it doesn't sound very appetizing. In any case, the trip was our way of celebrating all the seasons the Rounders had spent together, one last big adventure before the team broke up.

After thinking about it for weeks, I could hardly believe the day was almost here. Finally! I couldn't wait.

Wiping his hands on his apron, Dad disappeared into the den. He returned a few seconds later carrying a thick tan folder, which he dumped on the kitchen table. The folder contained all sorts of information he had collected for the trip: checklists of what to bring, camp-site reservations, maps, guides to plants and animals, a first-aid kit, magazine ads for the latest high-tech camping gear.

"You'd think you were launching an expedition to the moon instead of going on a camping trip," Mom said, eyeing the fat folder.

"Except there are no bears in space," said Stump. He picked up a pamphlet about how to survive a bear attack.

"Actually, there are a couple," Slingshot said. "Ursa Major and Ursa Minor. The great bear and the little bear."

"What are you talking about?" Stump asked.

"Constellations of stars," said Slingshot. "We call them the Big Dipper and the Little Dipper, but their official names are Ursa Major and Minor. 'Ursa' means bear in Latin." Slingshot knows all sorts of scientific facts. He wants to be a doctor when he grows up. Meanwhile, he does a pretty good impression of a human encyclopedia.

"Do they bite?" asked Stump.

"Of course not," said Slingshot.

"Exactly," said Stump. "We don't have to worry about them."

"The constellations can be pretty handy, actually. If you can spot the bears in the night sky, you can find the North Star. Once you know where that is, you can find your way out of the woods. If you ever get lost, these bears are your friends."

"So is GPS," Stump said. "My dad has it on his phone. He could look up our location, then we could call someone for a ride and tell them exactly where to pick us up."

"Assuming you could get a signal that deep in the woods," Slingshot muttered.

"We're not going to get lost," Dad said, spreading open a map of the North Woods on the table.

The park wasn't the kind of place with a playground and baseball diamonds. It was a huge nature reserve. A vast area of deep forests and craggy mountains that sprawled across parts of two states. Smack through the middle of it all ran the mighty Big Fork, represented on the map by a twisting blue ribbon. Here and there along its banks, little tent icons showed the locations of campsites.

"We'll take this road into the park," Dad said, pointing to a thin black line, "and follow it all the way to the lodge at Six Mile Cove. That's where we hit the water."

He wrote START next to the symbol for a boat ramp on the map.

"Then we paddle downstream through Whistling Gorge and around Elk Bend to the campsite at Tinkham Woods," I recited from memory. Dad and I had been poring over the map all summer.

"Exactly."

"What in the world is this place?" Stump asked, pointing to a spot farther down the river. "Devil's Furnace?"

"Mondo rapids," Dad said. "The biggest,

32

wildest stretch of white water on the river. We should hit it the morning of our second day."

"Why's it called Devil's Furnace?"

"They say the river runs so fast through there that it seems to boil." Dad traced his finger along the river. "All flat water after that."

"Dad," I said. "Aren't you forgetting something?"

He looked at me. He looked at the checklist on the table. "Sleeping bags, food, camp stove, life vests, fishing rods, hamburgers, bug juice. I think we've got it all covered."

"Dad," I prodded. "The legend."

"You mean that crazy nonsense about the highwayman?" He grinned. "They don't want to hear that."

"What legend?" the guys asked. "What's a highwayman? You mean the dude who sits in the little booth and collects tolls?"

"A highwayman is a bandit," I said with glee. "A robber."

"I guess if you really want to hear it . . ."

"We do!"

With a sigh, Dad closed the folder and launched into his story.

## THE DEVIL'S FURNACE

*A long, long time ago, way back in colonial times, a bandit plagued the north country. He would swoop out of the woods and rob coaches traveling the lonely roads at night, disappearing back into the forest before anyone could stop him. People grew fearful of venturing from their homes after dark.*

*In time, the thief, by now known as the Moonlight Bandit for his habit of attacking at night, grew bolder. He stopped waiting for coaches to pass along the road and started venturing into the villages to raid inns and taverns.*

*One cold, wet night, he waylaid a trader outside the tavern near Six Mile Cove, relieving the man of a bundle of* valuable furs and a bag of gold. The victim's cries alerted some villagers inside the tavern, and they pursued the bandit into the forest. The men tracked him to the bank of Big Fork River. But just when they thought they finally had him, he leaped into a hidden canoe and slipped away. The men quickly launched boats of their own and gave chase.

With justice hot on his heels, the thief reached the Devil's Furnace. In the driving rain, the water seethed and swelled like a boiling pot. There was no way he could get through the rapids in a heavily loaded birch-bark canoe. But his pursuers were gaining fast, so he took a deep breath and plunged ahead.

Unwilling to risk the rapids, the chase party paddled to the shore. As lightning flashed, they watched in horror as a whirlpool grabbed the highwayman's canoe and sucked it under, cargo and all.

*That was the last anyone ever saw of the*
*Moonlight Bandit. Anyone, that is, from*
*this world.*

"Whoa!" exclaimed Stump. "Is this true?"

"Wait," I said. "We're just getting to the good part."

Before I could say more, Mr. Bones bounded onto the sofa and buried his head in my lap. He likes scary stories as much as the next guy; he just needs a little coddling to make it to the end.

"Ahem." My dad cleared his throat. "May I continue?" We settled down, and he went on with the tale.

*According to legend, the current pulled*
*the thief down into a cavern deep within*
*the earth. It was a weird place, a vast*
*underground room, very hot, with walls*
*that seemed to pulse. At the far end of the*
*cave, a strange man dressed all in black*
*fed stones into a huge fireplace, whose*
*river rock chimney seemed to stretch*

upward for miles and miles. The soft, dull yellow stones hissed and smoldered as the man tossed them on the fire.

The highwayman blinked. He thought he must have been dreaming. "Who in the world are you?" he asked.

"Never mind about that," the stranger said, tossing another boulder on his fire. It released a cloud of horribly stinky smoke. "You've got a pack of aggrieved villagers to worry about."

"I am in a bit of a jam," admitted the thief. "Mind if I lie low down here for a spell?"

"Be my guest," said the stranger. "I ask only one thing in exchange."

"Name it."

"I get to keep a pelt from your fine collection. Any pelt I choose."

The brigand thought it over for a minute. He hated to give up one of the stolen furs. They were worth a lot of silver. On the other hand, he wasn't in much of a position to bargain.

"Deal," he agreed.

"Excellent," said the stranger, fire dancing in his deep, deep eyes. "You'll be safe in my chimney. No one will ever find you there."

"But I'll roast!" protested the bandit.

"Trust me," said the figure in black. "You won't feel a thing."

With that, he grabbed the highwayman and stuffed him up the chimney.

"Wait," shrieked the man as smoke engulfed him. "What about the skins? Spare me and you can keep them all!"

"I have the only hide I want," cackled the stranger. "Yours!"

To this day, when the wind is right, they say you can still hear the old thief howling inside a weird rock formation that rises out of the river at the very spot where he went under. People say the rocks are a chimney that vents an underground

*furnace, and that the devil is down there*
*still, stoking his fire to boil the river.*

"Love that story," I said. "Totally spooky."

"Rocks don't burn," Stump said stubbornly.

"It's a legend," I said. "It doesn't have to make sense."

"Brimstone burns," said Slingshot. "It also stinks to high heaven. Could be a vein of it running through the bedrock up at Abenaki."

"I just hope we don't run into that whirlpool," I said with a laugh. A slightly nervous laugh.

"Are you kidding?" Stump whooped. "I hope we do! There's gold down there. Real treasure! We ought to look for it!"

"I could go for that," I admitted. "Except for the part about drowning in a whirlpool. But lost treasure, yeah, that would be cool."

"Hot, you mean," said Slingshot. "It would be hot. We're talking about a place called the Devil's *Furnace*."

"Who cares about the temperature?" said Stump. "We find gold, you can buy an air-conditioner. Are you in or not?"

Slingshot and I looked at each other. As if we had any choice.

"Definitely!" we both exclaimed. Which is how our simple camping trip turned into a treasure hunt.

Dad chuckled.

"I wouldn't worry too much about the legend of the Moonlight Bandit," he said. "What concerns me is rain. Nothing's more miserable than camping in the rain. Let's hope we've seen the end of it."

Wow, I hadn't even thought of that. Dad was right. Rain would stink. I crossed my fingers and wished for the sky to stay clear.

Maybe I should have crossed my toes while I was at it.

# ★ CHAPTER 4 ★

The next morning, I got out of bed early and ran to the window to check the weather. The sky was bright. The birds sang. It looked like a beautiful day.

"Excellent," I said to Mr. Bones. "Our game against the Bixburg Bluebottles won't be canceled."

I dressed quickly and went downstairs for breakfast. Mom and Dad already sat at the kitchen table, drinking coffee and reading the newspaper. Rather, Dad was reading. Mom had a pencil and was working the sudoku puzzle.

"Morning, kid," they said.

Dad offered to make omelets. He loves whipping up omelets. The bigger the better, filled with more ingredients than your average grocery store. Usually I love to eat them. But today I wasn't that hungry. Game-day butterflies, I guess. I couldn't help but worry about Slingshot. Anyway, Dad would be camp cook during our trip. Plenty of time to eat a big breakfast then.

"I think I'll just have cereal," I said. I poured myself a bowl of Pirate Crunch, the kind with the little frosted cannonballs, and joined them at the table.

Dad look disappointed. He should open a restaurant. That way he could cook omelets all day long. And Mr. Bones could gobble up the leftovers.

"Mind giving me the sports section?" I asked.

Dad handed it over. "Knock yourself out," he said.

Above the fold on the front page was a

picture of Slingshot. He stood on the mound with a vacant look on his face, buckets of rain beating down.

Tiny writing underneath the picture said Gabby Hedron had taken the photograph. Gabby was my friend and classmate at Rambletown Elementary School. She covers the Rounders for the newspaper. Lately she's begun blogging for the website as well. But I still preferred to get my news the old-fashioned way: printed on paper that could be read over a bowl of Pirate Crunch cereal at breakfast. Besides, my mom didn't allow electronic devices at the table. Or food at the computer.

Gabby had written a story to go along with the picture.

## RAIN RIPS RAMBLETOWN

*A torrential storm washed out yesterday's playoff game between the Rambletown Rounders and the Lumleyville Lumberjacks. The freak cloudburst flooded the field,*

*swamped the grandstand, and sent players
and fans alike scrambling for cover.*

*Like the weather, pitcher Slingshot
Slocum was all wet. At one point he walked
three straight batters. All day long he pitched
like a blindfolded man at dinner. He couldn't
find the plate. Considering how generous he
was with the free passes, the rain was a good
thing. Thanks to it, the game was called in
the fifth inning with the Rounders leading
by a run, and so the home team escaped
with a win. They live another day. Let's hope
both the sun and Slingshot shine for the next
game.*

I pushed the paper aside, wondering if Slingshot had seen the story yet. One thing about
Gabby, she didn't pull any punches. Once when
I was stuck in a horrible hitting slump, she had
written that I played baseball like the pendu-
lum of a clock. I swung and swung and never
hit anything. I laughed about it now, but at the

time my feelings were really hurt. The thing is, Gabby loved the Rounders. I don't think anyone rooted harder for us than she did, or felt worse when we lost. Maybe that explained why she was so tough on us. I hoped Slingshot wouldn't take the story too hard.

"Nice day for a game," Mom said, rousing me from my thoughts.

"Looks like it," I said.

"You guys home or away today?" Dad asked.

"Away," I said. "Bixburg."

"They have that good pitcher, don't they? What's his name again?"

"Harrison 'Big Train' Blain," I told him. "Really wicked stuff. Plus, the catcher is Slats Connolly and Choo-Choo Choo plays center-field. They call Choo-Choo the Steam Engine, he runs so fast. Both guys are All-Stars. Big Train would be, too, except Flicker Pringle owns the pitcher's spot."

"Tough team," said Dad. "Good luck."

"If we win," I said, "we'll be just one game

away from going back to the championship."

"Can I give you a ride to the game?" Mom offered.

I smiled at her. She always asked if I wanted a ride. And I always turned her down. The thing is, ever since I was old enough to play for the Rounders, I've ridden my bike to Rambletown Park to pick up the team bus for road games. Always. It's a routine that never changes. Because in baseball, routines are everything. Like I've said, if you mess with them, only bad things can happen.

"No thanks." I turned her down.

"Figured there's no harm in asking," Mom said. Just as she always did. "I guess I'll see you there in the second inning."

Arriving late to games was another tradition. Once upon a time, Mom and Dad always came early. Then one day they missed the first inning of a game, and I ended up hitting everything in sight. Four trips to the plate, four home runs.

That's when people started calling me Walloper.

And when Mom and Dad started showing up
late on purpose.

"Perfect," I said.

"Before you go this afternoon," Dad said,
"would you do me a favor? Would you start getting some things together for our trip?"

He handed me a list. Typewritten. Single-
spaced. Dad had been a Boy Scout as a kid. He
still lived by the motto Be prepared.

"There's nothing I'd love more," I said.
"Thanks!"

If he got my sarcasm, he didn't show it:

"Great. I knew I could count on you."

I spent the rest of the morning up in the
attic over our garage. There was a ton of stuff
up there. A lot of it was banged up or just plain
broken. Some of it seemed to date back to the
time of the dinosaurs. All of it was covered with
dust.

I found my old tricycle, several ancient pairs

of ice skates, and the car seat my parents made me sit in when I was little. I had hated that thing. It was impossible to buckle. There was a fishing rod missing its reel, three patio chairs (one still had all four legs attached to it), a wooden tennis racket with no strings, a collection of bamboo rakes, and a blown-out umbrella. I opened the umbrella, black with a wooden handle. Some of the metal spokes were bent, and there were a couple small tears in the fabric. Briefly I considered rescuing it. Maybe I could patch it. You never knew, an umbrella might come in handy if we had any more storms. Then I thought better of it. If the rain washed down again like it had yesterday, we'd need something a lot bigger than a mangled umbrella to stay dry. We'd need the Houston Astrodome: a ballpark with a roof over it. I closed up the umbrella and started poking around some more.

After peering into box after cardboard box (loads of Christmas decorations) and bag after plastic trash bag (outgrown clothes, mostly), I eventually stumbled upon a stash of camping gear and started sifting through it. As I worked, a nagging little thought kept trying to form in my mind. Something I'd heard once, something about umbrellas. I ignored it and made a pile of the stuff on Dad's list.

Three-person nylon tent in a green drawstring bag. Check. Cooking pots. Check. Rolled-up sleeping bags. Check. Mosquito netting, collapsible cooler for food and drinks, refillable water jugs. Check, check, and check.

Before I knew it, my mom was calling my name from somewhere down in the garage, telling me lunch was ready. Time flies when you're having fun. Also, it flies when you're rummaging through a hot attic stuffed with more artifacts than the Smithsonian.

"How's it going?" she asked. "Finding everything?"

I looked at the stack I'd made. It was practically as tall as I was.

"I think it's all here," I said, wondering how

in the world we'd fit everything into a canoe. Well, Dad probably had a plan. He always did.

I climbed down into the garage, where the temperature was about a thousand degrees cooler than in the attic. Then I went into the house and washed up for lunch: two PB&J sandwiches chased by a couple glasses of milk.

Do you know there once was a major leaguer by the name of Wade Boggs who supposedly only ate chicken? He claimed it made him hit better. True story. His exact words were, "There's hits in chicken." He even published a book of his favorite recipes. Boggs won the American League batting title five times, so maybe he was right about chicken. Or maybe he was just a really great hitter with bizarre eating habits. Anyway, I guess peanut butter and jelly is my chicken. I always eat it for lunch before playing. Baloney I save for after certain games. The bad ones.

When I finished eating, I felt ready for baseball. I quickly changed into my uniform, pulled on my cap, white with a red R for Rambletown, and clattered out the door. With my mitt hooked over the handlebars of my bike and Mr. Bones trotting beside me, I set out for Rambletown Park.

"Good luck, Banjie," Mom called from the porch. "See you in the second inning!"

Halfway to the field, it hit me. The umbrella thing that had been bothering me. It had to do with luck. Not the good kind.

Specifically, opening an umbrella inside a house was supposed to make bad luck rain down. One of those old superstitions like breaking a mirror or walking under a ladder.

"Uh-oh," I said out loud, my grip tightening on the handlebars.

Now that I thought about it, hadn't I seen a mirror up there with all the other junk? What about a ladder? But I hadn't touched the mirror, had I? I couldn't have cracked it. And never in a million years would I be foolish enough to walk under a ladder. Then again, I definitely had opened the umbrella. Holy moley! If I'd known the attic was going to be such a mine-field, I never would have gone up there in the first place.

I wondered if the garage counted as part of the house.

I hoped not.

# ★ CHAPTER 5 ★

As I cruised up to Rambletown Field, I saw that the playing area had drained nicely overnight. Not much more than a foot of water covered the grass. A flock of ducks paddled around on Rambletown's newest lake. Who needed the Big Fork River? We could go rafting right here. Some kids were feeding the ducks stale bread from brown paper bags. The sight reminded me of the grasshopper infestation we'd suffered earlier in the season. I'll take ducks over grasshoppers any day of the week. For one thing, ducks don't eat grass. For another, their quacking is positively quiet compared to the buzzing of grasshoppers. Those grasshoppers sounded like jet engines.

Anyway, as long as we didn't get hit with any more major storms, the puddle would soon dry up. By the time we got back from our trip, the field would be dry and the ducks would be gone. Meanwhile, we had a game to play in Bixburg.

The bus stood waiting at the curb. My teammates were scrambling aboard. Several called out greetings.

"Move it!" yelled Gilly. "You're almost late!"

Skip Lou Clementine has this thing about time. In his book, "on time" means early and everything else counts as late.

Standing on the pedals to get up more speed, I waved. Big mistake. I never saw the pothole coming. I rode smack into it at about fifty miles an hour. My front tire jammed into the hole, and I flipped over the handlebars like a rodeo cowboy getting tossed by a bucking bull. I landed on my butt, facing the opposite direction of where I'd been going.

"Ouch!" I said.

Mr. Bones ran over and licked my face. My friends raced over after him. I found myself staring up into a sea of alarmed faces.

"Pffft," I said, getting to my feet. "I'm okay."

Pure coincidence? Or was the umbrella already taking its revenge?

The guys broke into loud applause as I picked myself up and dusted off my uniform. Aside from feeling like a goofball, I wasn't hurt.

"Nice trick," said Glove Rodriquez. "Where'd you learn that one?"

"You want me to teach it to you?" I offered, wheeling my bike over to the rack and chaining it.

Laughing, we hurried onto the bus.

Mr. Bones led us to the wide bench seat all the way in the back. As I moved down the aisle behind him, I slapped hands with my teammates. Then Mr. Bones jumped up on the seat between Stump and Slingshot, and Glove and I squeezed down next to them.

Once we were settled, Skip Lou cranked the bus into gear, and we hit the road for Bixburg.

"Are you really okay?" Slingshot asked. "You did a full front flip with a twist!"

"I'm fine," I said. "How're you? How's your arm?"

"Never better," Slingshot said. He looked up with a scowl. Gabby was sitting directly in front of us, her brown ponytail sticking out the back of her Rounders cap. "I can't wait to pitch," he declared.

Gabby shifted in her seat. She turned and faced us.

"Umm . . . about the story in today's paper," she hemmed.

"Was there a story?" Stump interrupted. "I didn't see it. Journalism is going downhill, if you ask me." He crossed his arms and glared at the reporter.

"Oh, there was a story all right," Slingshot said.

Gabby's face flushed.

"Easy, guys," I said. "Gabby didn't mean anything. She just has a, ah, you know . . . a forceful way of writing. Right, Gabby?"

The bus got really quiet. Everybody turned around in their seats and stared at us. More specifically, they stared at Gabby. Nobody looked very forgiving.

*Uh-oh,* I thought. My attempt at playing peacemaker wasn't exactly working. I tried again. "Remember that time you said I should stick to Whiffle ball, because all I did was whiff?" I forced a chuckle.

Gabby's face turned a little redder.

"Yeah, and once you compared Velcro to a human battering ram because he kept smashing into the outfield wall," added Stump. "What was up with that?"

"Or how about the time," piped up Gasser from across the aisle, "you put a picture of Stump making a throwing error in the paper? You said his arm was like the identity of the Lone Ranger: a total mystery."

By now Gabby was beet red. And the rest of us were giggling. Even Slingshot. You had to admit, her stories were pretty funny. Maybe if she hadn't been the Rounders' biggest fan, we could have held her words against her. But in our hearts we knew she really, really wanted us to do well.

"I didn't mean to make fun," she said. "I'm really sorry for hurting your feelings, Slingshot."

"Forget about it," Slingshot said. "It wasn't my best game."

"Tomorrow you can write about how many strikeouts he gets today," I said. "He's going to twist the Bluebottles into pretzels."

"I'd like that," Gabby said with relief. "And then it's one more game until a rematch with the Haymakers, right? Oh, man, I hope you get back to the championship and whip them. I can't stand those guys, they're so full of themselves."

"We're sure going to try," I said loudly. Up

and down the bus, the guys nodded. It looked like a fishing derby, there was so much bobbing going on.

With that, we pulled into Bixburg Memorial Park and hustled off the bus and onto the field to get ready for the game.

The sky was like a freshly washed window as we took batting practice: perfectly clear. The sun shone down warmly, trees at the edge of the field swayed in a gentle breeze, and the chatter of fans floated across the diamond from the sidelines of the Bluebottles' plain, well-tended field. I always enjoyed our visits to Bixburg. Especially when we won.

After we each had a turn at the plate, Skip Lou called us over to the bench for a quick pep talk.

"One down and two to go, guys," he said as we formed a circle around him. "I know you're all thinking about the championship. But let me tell you, you can't beat the Haymakers today. So let's not get ahead of ourselves. Let's just go out

**59**

there and do our best against the Bluebottles. Have fun and play the way you know how." He held out his hand.

We all thrust ours into the circle.

"One, two, three," we chanted. "Go Rounders!"

Ducks, our leadoff hitter, clapped a helmet on his head and grabbed a bat.

"BATTER UP!" roared the ump from behind home plate.

With that, the game began.

Pitching for the Bluebottles, Big Train Blain started Ducks with a two-speed changeup. It came out of his hand fast, then seemed to hit the brakes halfway home. Ducks stood no chance against that backpedaling ball. He swung and missed by a mile. Our left fielder managed to lay some wood on Big Train's next offering, but the Bixburg third baseman scooped his worm burner and gunned to first for the out. Stump came up next and looked at a ball and two blazing strikes before getting hoodwinked by another changeup. Just like that, we had two outs.

I took my favorite Louisville Slugger from Billy Wishes, rubbed the batboy's head for luck, and strode up to the plate.

"Wait for your pitch, kid," Skip Lou yelled as I took a couple of practice cuts. "One is all it takes."

Big Train kicked and delivered. Coming out of his hand, the pitch looked like a fastball. But I wasn't buying it. I knew it would slam on the brakes eventually. I waited an extra beat, then let it rip.

CRACK!

I didn't quite get all of the ball, but I got enough to bounce it into a cluster of fans sitting in folding chairs down the left-field line for a ground-rule double. If my blast bothered Big Train, he didn't let on. Instead, he whiffed Tugboat on a series of pitches so slippery they made ice look like flypaper. Some real ice would have been nice. Tugboat could have used it to nurse his bruised ego. The way things were going, we might all need some.

The Bluebottles jogged in to hit, and we trotted out to play defense.

As Slingshot fired his warm-up tosses to Tugboat, a few wispy gray clouds drifted into the sky that until then had been so blue.

I looked up and frowned. "Where did these come from?" I wondered. "Go on, beat it, clouds!"

The clouds did not listen to me. Instead, they called over some friends for a party. In a matter of minutes, the sun made like invisible ink and vanished. You could've traded a hundred-dollar bill for nothing but pennies and the change wouldn't have been greater.

A real hundred-dollar bill would have been nice. We could have used it to buy rain slickers. All of a sudden, it sure looked like we were going to need them.

"BATTER UP!" barked the ump.

# ★ CHAPTER 6 ★

Tugboat flashed the sign. Inside fastball. He made a target out of his big mitt. Up on the mound, Slingshot nodded and brought his hands together to begin his wind-up.

"C'mon now, kid! Fire it in there!" I urged.

Slingshot delivered. The pitch came in fast. Fast and high. Really high. Tugboat leaped up and snatched the ball before it sailed to the backstop.

"BALL ONE!" grunted the ump as the first fat raindrops began to fall.

"Nice and easy," I called as Tugboat rifled the ball back to Slingshot. "Hit the target."

Slingshot toed the rubber. He wound up

and threw another pitch.

"BALL TWO!" barked the umpire as the ball bounced in the dirt a foot in front of home plate.

*Uh-oh*, I thought. *The forkball again.*

The rain came down a little harder.

Two pitches later, the Bluebottles' leadoff man trotted to first base with a four-pitch walk and the rain really started to spritz.

The umpire looked at the sky. I did the same. Off in the distance the sun was shining. Directly overhead was a different story. A whole different language, even. The sky above the ball field was one big gray bowl of soup. The ump shrugged and motioned the next batter to the plate.

"PLAY BALL!" he cried.

I guess he hoped it was just a passing shower. I know I did.

Slingshot bounced another pitch, and the runner on first scampered down to second. As it turned out, he could've saved himself the trouble of stealing. Slingshot tossed three more balls, and all of a sudden the Bluebottles had players on first and second with no outs.

I thought back to our last game. Slingshot had now walked five batters in a row. I couldn't remember another time in all the years we'd played together that he had ever done that.

"Settle down now, Slingshot," I called. "Let's turn two, guys!"

To my left, Stump nodded and pounded his mitt. "Turn two!" he echoed, knowing that a double play was a pitcher's best friend.

We never got the chance to flash our leather. Slingshot missed by a mile with his next pitch. The ball caromed past Tugboat, slithered all the way to the backstop, and both base runners advanced. Another wild pitch followed, allowing the runners to race home. The score was now 2–0. Worse, the rain was really starting to pound.

The umpire shook his head. He had seen enough. He pulled off his mask and signaled a delay.

"Let's wait a few minutes and see if it clears," he said. "I hate to postpone a playoff game." Then he trotted off to the parking lot and ducked inside his car. Fans streamed after him.

*Here we go again,* I thought as I jogged off the field. Part of me wished I'd brought that old umbrella from the attic, because Bixburg didn't have a covered dugout. Another part wished I'd never seen the rotten thing. Or opened it.

My teammates and I gathered up our mitts and bats and balls and stuffed them into Skip Lou's huge canvas duffel bag to keep everything dry. Then we huddled together, shirts pulled over our heads like turtle shells, and tried to cheer up Slingshot.

Our friend wore a stunned expression on his face. His mouth hung open and his eyes stared blankly. He looked like a fish that couldn't believe the worm it had just eaten was attached to a hook. A real hook would've been nice. If the rain got any heavier, the baseball diamond would turn into a lake and we could use the hook to catch dinner.

At least Slingshot seemed to understand that play had been suspended. He wasn't standing on the mound insisting everything was fine, like he had during the downpour against Lumleyville. In a storm of bad luck and weird happenings, this was the only glimmer of sunshine.

"Forget about it," I told him. "We're only down by two." I wondered if now would be a good time to mention the umbrella I'd found in the attic. I decided against it. No reason to give everybody something else to worry about.

"Once this rain stops," said Velcro, "we'll go right back out there and win the game."

Slingshot didn't say anything. He just stood there looking like a careless electrician: shocked. Mr. Bones jumped up and tried to lick his face. Slingshot didn't seem to notice. My dog barked and barked, then ran out onto the diamond and began circling the bases.

Skip joined our huddle.

"The ump will give the rain ten minutes," he said. "If it doesn't clear up by then, we're looking at a makeup game."

I nodded. If these fluky downpours kept up, we'd never get through the playoffs. Every time we played, the rain poured down and the game got suspended. Our season was starting to feel like an airport during the holidays: nothing but delays and cancellations. A real airport would have been nice. It would be full of radar and all the latest weather-forecasting equipment. We could have used it to find out when rain was coming and scheduled our games for different days.

As Skip Lou spoke and the guys grumbled about the lousy rain, Mr. Bones continued to dart around the bases, yapping.

"Quiet down, boy!" I called to him. "We're having a team meeting over here."

Mr. Bones barked even louder. I shrugged and excused myself from the huddle to go get him. As I trotted onto the diamond, I noticed something funny. I looked up. My face did not get soaked. As I watched, the clouds evaporated before my eyes and the sun broke through.

"It stopped!" I shouted. "The rain has stopped."

Mr. Bones ran over and leaped up, planting two muddy paws on my chest. He barked in my face, then licked it. In dog language, I think the barks meant, "No duh, Sherlock! What do you think I've been trying to tell you?"

Out in the parking lot, car doors slammed as the ump and all the fans hurried back to the field. All except my parents, that is. It was still the first inning, after all. They'd be out there awhile longer. I smiled and waved to them.

"All right!" said Skip Lou. "Guys, we're back in business. Ready to try again, Slingshot?"

Our pitcher did not answer.

I looked over at my friend. His arms were tightly crossed over his chest. He stared at his cleats.

"Slingshot?" asked Skip Lou. "What's up, buddy? Game on. We need a pitcher."

Finally Slingshot made eye contact. "Umm, my arm doesn't feel so great, Skip," he said. "I think it tightened up during the delay."

Skip Lou studied him closely. It wasn't like Slingshot to turn down the ball.

"You sure?" the coach asked.

Slingshot nodded. A dismal little duck of his head.

"Okay, let's see," Skip said, checking his clipboard. "I guess Gasser could come in to pitch and Velcro could take his place in center. Are you sure you want to come out, Slingshot? You know you can't go back in later."

Another woeful nod.

Skip reported our lineup changes to the ump, and the Rounders ran out onto the field. All except Slingshot, who grabbed some pine on the bench.

Gasser tossed a few warm-up pitches. No one was going to confuse him with Cy Young, but at least his throws wound up in the same zip code as the strike zone. After his fifth toss, the umpire nodded.

"PLAY BALL!" he commanded.

A Bixburg batter stepped to the plate, the same guy who had been up there before the rain. The count was two balls and no strikes. The bases were empty. The score was 2–0.

Gasser fired a fastball. The batter let it go.

"STEE-RIKE ONE!" hollered the ump.

The hitter swung at the next pitch, sizzling a grounder across the infield. Gilly dived to his right at first and speared the ball, then back-handed it to Gasser, who had raced over from the mound to cover first base.

"OUT!" boomed the ump.

"Way to be alert, guys!" I called from third as Gasser headed back to the hill.

The play must have gotten Gasser's adrenaline flowing, because he absolutely overpowered the next two batters, striking out one of them and getting the other to pop weakly to the Glove at second base.

"Rock it, Gasser!" I shouted.

We trotted off the field to take our cuts, glad to have stopped the bleeding. If Gasser could keep pitching like this, we'd at least have a chance. We would, that is, if we could derail Big Train. The kid picked up right where he'd left off in the first, setting down Gasser, Gilly, and Velcro in order.

Before we knew it, we were out in the field again. Gasser continued to pitch well in the bottom of the inning, giving up only a harmless double to Slats Connolly, Bixburg's top power hitter.

In the third, Big Train seemed on his way to another one-two-three inning. He whiffed Ocho and the Glove and had Ducks in a 0–2 hole, when our left fielder caught a piece of a straight fast-ball and raced down to first with a hit.

"Way to go, Ducks!" we cheered.

Stump followed with a bloop base hit to short center.

"Ducks on the pond," called the guys on the bench. "Bring them home, Walloper!"

"Ducks on the pond" is baseball lingo for runners on base. The only real Ducks out there was Bunion, and there was no pond for miles. Back in Rambletown, sure. But here in Bixburg, it was nice and dry now that the showers had passed.

In any case, I sure meant to try to plate those runners.

# ★ CHAPTER 7 ★

**B**ig Train wound up and delivered. I saw the ball leave his hand and guessed fastball. The way it rolled off his fingers just looked right, straight and hard and nothing sneaky about it.

I swung.

*CRACK!*

This time I got all of it. The ball flew off my bat and didn't come down until I was rounding second base. I tucked my head and charged for third, where Skip Lou waved for me to keep going.

I did, sliding home under the tag of Slats Connolly to wild cheers from my teammates.

Just like that, we led 3 to 2.

"That's why we call him Walloper!" shouted Billy.

Man, I love that kid.

We scored another run on back-to-back doubles by Tugboat and Gasser, before Big Train ended our little hit party by spinning three off-speed pitches past Gilly. The Bluebottles ran in to bat, and we took their places in the field, happy to be staked to a lead. Teams didn't often score four runs off Big Train. Certainly not in one inning. Now we just had to make our lead stand up.

In the bottom half, Big Train cracked a lead-off homer. The guy was having a monster game. Fortunately for us, Gasser wasn't doing too bad himself. He recovered to retire the next three batters.

Neither team scored in the fourth or fifth, so we entered the sixth and final frame leading 4 to 3.

Gasser got us off to a good start with a high

hopper to third that he beat out for a single. Gilly moved him to second with a bunt but was thrown out at first by Slats. Velcro came up next and scorched a frozen rope to center. Choo-Choo Choo one-hopped it and quickly fired the ball to the cutoff man, holding Velcro to a single. Gasser advanced to third on the play. With one down and runners at the corners, Ocho stepped to the plate and the Glove moved into the on-deck circle. I was on triple deck.

"Come on, Ocho!" I hollered. "Let's add some insurance runs!"

Working from the stretch to hold our runners close, Big Train uncorked his famous slip-gear reverse changeup yeast ball. I'd seen him throw it before. Just never in a game. The thing was sick. It started low and slow, only to gain speed and rise up as it motored homeward, hence the name yeast ball.

After looking at regular changeups in his earlier at-bats, Ocho wasn't prepared for the sudden burst of speed. He swung way late and nubbed a dribbler.

Slats pounced on the ball and gunned it to first for an easy out. The minute he threw, Gasser sprinted for home from third.

"Suicide!" screamed Slats, scrambling to block the plate. The first baseman whipped the ball back to him. Mud spraying from his cleats, Gasser slid. Slats reached to apply the tag. From the bench, it was too close to call.

The ump had a better view. Unfortunately, what he saw was not what we wanted.

"OUT!" he roared.

I picked up my fielder's mitt and trotted to third. Unless we went to extra innings, I wouldn't get another chance to hit in this game. Which was fine with me. I'd gladly trade a trip to the plate in the future for a win right now.

"Let's go, guys!" I shouted as the last half of the sixth inning got under way. "One, two, three."

Gasser toed the rubber, then fired a fastball. The Bluebottle batter clocked it to deep left field, where Ducks chased it down and made a leaping catch. One pitch, one out.

"That's the stuff," called Skip Lou from the bench. "Look alive, guys!"

The second batter belted the ball even harder than the first one had. His towering shot would have cleared the wall at Ramble-town Field for a game-tying homer. Lucky for us, the Bixburg outfield doesn't have a fence. It just keeps going. Velcro put down his head and ran.

And ran.

And ran.

About halfway to Kalamazoo, he finally caught up to it and put it away for out number two.

"Great catch!" I yelled.

I doubt Velcro heard me. He was miles away. We waited for him to trot back into position. The wait was good. It gave Gasser a chance to rest. Either he was getting tired, or the Blue-bottles were getting stronger. Pick your poison.

We needed to end this thing before somebody hit a bomb.

"BATTER UP!" barked the ump as Velcro finally arrived back in center field.

"One more out, Gasser!" I called. "That's all we need!"

Gasser nodded and delivered a curveball. At least I think it was supposed to be a curveball. It didn't actually curve, though. It hung out over the plate, big and fat and just begging to be pulverized. The batter swung like the ball was a potato and he meant to mash it.

*CRACK!*

It flew into the sky high above right field. The Bixburg fans rose with it, leaping to their feet and roaring. Ocho drifted back, way back. The runner chugged around the bases. As he crossed second, the ball reached the peak of its flight and began to plunge back to earth like a meteor. It plummeted so fast you expected to see flames. If it landed, it was a home run for sure. A homer and probably a mile-deep crater.

If I were a dinosaur, I would've kissed my loved ones good-bye.

For a frozen instant, the ball and Ocho converged on the horizon. Then the center fielder tumbled across the grass. By now, the batter had crossed home plate and jumped into the arms of his celebrating teammates. Then Ocho popped to his feet. He pulled the ball out of his mitt and waved it over his head. From where I stood by third base, it was hard to tell if the ball was actually smoking. It didn't matter. What counted was that he had stolen a downtowner from the Bluebottles for out number three.

The Bixburg fans fell silent. It was our turn to cheer now. We had beaten the Bluebottles and kept ourselves alive in the chase for the championship.

As we gathered up our stuff, I couldn't help wondering if we'd won the game but lost something bigger. Namely, our best pitcher. I'd never seen Slingshot in such a funk. We needed him to make like a pole vaulter and get over it. And we needed him to do it fast.

I glanced over my shoulder and saw Gabby standing off to one side of the team bus. Tongue pinched between her teeth, she scribbled in her notebook. She looked up and caught my eye. Right away I could tell she was thinking the same thing I was.

If we couldn't count on Slingshot, the Haymakers would eat us for lunch. Assuming we even made it to the championship. Which was a pretty big assumption considering how lucky we'd been to avoid disaster in the last couple games.

Gabby shrugged her shoulders and returned to her scribbling. I climbed onto the bus and took my usual seat in back with Mr. Bones and the guys. Gabby boarded last and stayed up front.

With Skip Lou behind the wheel, the bus pulled out of the parking lot. All the way home, everybody kept really quiet. You never would have guessed we'd just won a playoff game. The ride felt more like a math test than a victory celebration. It was hushed and tense, everyone thinking hard.

Real math would have been nice. Slingshot, for one, could have used a review of the number three. As in three strikes, three outs, three wins in the playoffs to earn a trip to the championship. Three was our magic number.

I just hoped Slingshot could find the magic in his right arm. If he didn't, all the math in the world would not help us. Our number would be up.

# ★ CHAPTER 8 ★

The next morning, I dashed outside to check the weather. Mr. Bones bounded through the kitchen door with me and raced to the end of the driveway. Few things get him going like a morning walk.

For my part, few things make me happier than sunshine on a game day. And so I was feeling pretty darn warm and fuzzy as I scooped the newspaper off the black-top: There was not a cloud in the sky. With a cheerful whistle, I opened the paper to the sports section.

Gabby had written another story.

# WEATHER WARRIORS

*The Rounders avoided disaster in Bixburg yesterday, overcoming a freak cloudburst to defeat the Bluebottles by a score of four to three. One more win punches Rambletown's ticket to the championship game, where the mighty Haymakers likely await.*

*Everybody pitched in for yesterday's victory. Gasser Phipps took over for staff ace Slingshot Slocum after a first-inning rain delay and threw gallantly in relief. The Great Walloper clocked a three-run homer. Outfielders Ducks Bunion, Velcro Ramirez, and Ocho James played incredible defense to preserve victory.*

*A win against the Windsor Gaskets this afternoon puts the Rounders within spitting distance of their second straight divisional title.*

*Let's just hope the weird weather doesn't rain on their parade.*

*Nice work, Gabby,* I thought. She'd captured the gist of the game without slamming Slingshot. I'd have to thank her.

I also needed to talk to Slingshot. After yesterday's game, his confidence was like the legendary continent of Atlantis. Lost. We needed to help him find it. If we didn't, our season would be like Atlantis, too. Sunk.

I went inside to eat breakfast with my parents. The radio was playing and I recognized the voice of Louie the Lip.

"You're listening to HOT 102.5," the DJ purred. "Before we return to music, here's today's AccuWeather forecast. Mostly clear skies this morning, with a chance of scattered showers. Afternoon thunderstorms are possible."

*Great,* I thought. *Just what we need. Scattered storms. Slingshot scattering harmless hits would be more like it.*

"You boys ready?" Mom asked.

"For Windsor?" I asked, handing her the paper. She took out the section with the daily sudoku puzzle and handed the rest to my dad.

Windsor fielded a strong team with a few great players, including a catcher by the name of Daniel "The Dervish" Luft. Kid moved like an octopus behind the plate. He always seemed to be wearing eight gloves, his long arms stretching this way and that to snag every pop fly and foul tip.

Mom looked up from her puzzle.

"For your trip," she said. "You leave first thing in the morning, isn't that the plan?"

"Sure is," said Dad. "We'll load up the van tonight after the game and head out at dawn."

"So you're all packed?" Mom asked.

"Almost," Dad said.

Mom narrowed her eyes. "Almost?"

"The gear's all set, thanks to Banjie's work in the attic. I just have to toss some clothes in a bag."

"When do you plan to do that?"

Dad drained his coffee and stood up. "Before we leave?" he said, making his statement a question.

"You're impossible!" Mom sighed. "Banjie?" She looked at me.

"I'll finish packing this morning."

Dad shot me a wink. "Good man," he said. He kissed Mom, gave me a pat on the back, and left for the office.

After breakfast I went upstairs and stuffed some clothes into a backpack. I tried to choose wisely. I didn't want to be the guy who capsized a raft because he brought too much junk. Two T-shirts, a pair of shorts, swim trunks, and a sweatshirt and blue jeans in case it got chilly at night. After packing, I changed into my Rounders uniform. Then I carried the backpack downstairs and dropped it in the mudroom, next to my sleeping bag. I was good to go.

"Did you remember your toothbrush?" Mom called from the kitchen.

Oops. I had not. Then again, if I packed it away now, what would I use tonight and in the morning?

"I still need it," I said.

"Good point," Mom said. "I'll remind you in the morning."

"Since I'm done, would it be all right if I went over to Slingshot's until game time, with Stump and Velcro?" I asked.

The guys and I wanted to try to cheer up Slingshot. If he could just forget about his pitching problems for a while, maybe they would make like a rainbow and fade away. A real rainbow would have been nice. It would have meant no more storms.

"What about lunch?" Mom asked.

Have you ever noticed how much time meals take up? Sometimes it seems like the whole day is divided between thinking about them, making them, and eating them. It's kind of boring. Sometimes I wish you could just swallow a magic pill or something. A vitamin that tasted great and filled you like an entire meal would be a good invention. Somebody should look into it.

"I can probably grab lunch at Slingshot's.

His parents won't mind."

Slingshot's mom and dad are both teachers. They have the whole summer off. Whenever I'm at his house and lunchtime rolls around, they always ask if I want to eat with them.

Usually I say yes. Unless lunch is an eggplant salad or something. Slingshot's parents have a garden and grow a lot of vegetables. No offense to Mrs. Slocum, but eggplant is gross.

"You may go," Mom said. "But don't invite yourself to eat over, okay? If you can see they're busy, come back home."

"Definitely," I said. "Thanks."

I grabbed my mitt, got my bike out of the garage, and headed down the street. Mr. Bones trotted beside me.

When we got to Stump's, my friend threw open the door before I even had a chance to knock. He was dressed for the game. Probably he'd slept in his uniform.

"Walloper!" he shouted. "Where have you been all morning? You've got to get me out of here! I can't take it anymore."

"Can't take what?" I asked.

Stump squinched up his face and started rattling off questions. "Did you remember bug spray? Socks? Clean underwear? Something to read, a bar of soap, your toothbrush, your retainer?"

"You should wait to pack your toothbrush," I said. "You'll need it before we leave."

"That's exactly what I told my mom," Stump said. "What is it with toothbrushes?"

"What did she say?"

"She just kept going with the questions." He resumed the rat-a-tat delivery: "Swim trunks, a towel, a flashlight, flip-flops, a hairbrush, your pillow, your head?"

I laughed. "Who brings pillows camping?"

"Like I said, I've got to get out of here."

Just then his mom walked into the front hall from the back of the house. She looked like she could use a break, too. Her face was red, as if she'd been arguing, and her hair had come loose from the band she wore, so that it stuck out all over the place.

"Hi, Mrs. Plumwhiff," I greeted her.

"Walloper," she said, "will you please take my son away from here? We've been going at it hammer and tongs all morning. Trying to get him to pack is like herding cats. I'll bet your mom doesn't have to nag you."

I thought it best not to answer.

"Mom!" exclaimed Stump. "I'm finished. Everything's ready. I'm done."

She put her hands on her hips. "Done? Everything you need for two days in the woods is packed? You know what? Don't even answer that. Just go."

Stump sighed heavily.

"And Stump?"

"Yes, Mom?"

"I love you." She smiled.

"Love you, too, Mom."

"Now get out of here and go win your game!"

With that, we bolted out the door, mounted

our bikes, and took off for Velcro's. As we ped-
aled, I snuck a look at the sky. I couldn't help it.
The unpredictable rain was beginning to make
me paranoid.

"You too, huh?" Stump asked.

"Me too what?" I said, playing dumb.

"You're wondering how the sky can be so
clear one minute and the next it's raining cats
and . . ." He glanced down at Mr. Bones, who
was bounding alongside his front tire. "Umm,
you know, raining like the end of the world."

"The question had crossed my mind," I
admitted.

"I think he's making his own rain," Stump
said. "I think Slingshot's a rainmaker."

"That's insane," I said.

"How would you explain it, then? Every time
he pitches, we get soaked!"

We wheeled up to Velcro's house. The center
fielder was tossing a baseball against a pitch-
back in his front yard. He speared a line drive
behind his back and waved. The kid was a

magician with his glove.

"We're going to Slingshot's until game time," I told him. "Can you come?"

"Let me ask," he said. "You guys want a drink or anything?"

"I'm good," I said.

"Me too," Stump said.

"Then I'll be right back." Velcro disappeared into the house.

Stump and I got off our bikes and started a game of catch. Mr. Bones ran back and forth between us, leaping at the ball.

"You should teach him to slide," Stump suggested. "Then we could play pickle."

"Dogs don't play pickle," I said, firing the ball. "They don't even eat them."

Stump caught the ball and whizzed it back. "But Mr. Bones is no ordinary dog," he insisted. "I bet he could learn. After all, he *is* a royal Oxford sniffing spaniel."

I cracked up. There's no such thing as a royal Oxford sniffing spaniel. Mr. Bones is a lovable mutt. But one time when a snooty lady in Hog City said he looked like a rat, Gasser Phipps told her he was, in fact, a very rare and expensive kind of dog called a royal Oxford sniffing spaniel. Gasser just made up the name on the spot. He claimed that in ancient times royal Oxfords had been bred to sniff the food of English kings for poison, which is why their noses were so long. The lady was blown away. She loved the idea of royal Oxford sniffing spaniels so much, she offered to buy Mr. Bones on the spot for one thousand dollars. People in Hog City have a lot of money.

It was a good joke. What made it even better was that the woman in question just happened to be Flicker Pringle's mother.

"He's not for sale," I'd told her. "Not even for a million dollars."

The door opened and Velcro galloped down the steps, wearing his uniform.

"Let's hit it," he said.

We jumped back on our bikes and rode

around the corner toward Slingshot's.

"By the way," I said. "Stump thinks Slingshot can make rain."

Velcro looked surprised. "He should wait until after the game to do it," he said.

"Good point," I agreed.

"I didn't say Slingshot *wants* to make rain," Stump said. "I said he's a RAINMAKER. Big difference. I think he's so gloomy about his terrible pitching that he's actually spewing negative energy into the air. All those bad thoughts somehow ionize the atmosphere and cause these massive downpours."

"Nuts," I said as we rode up to Slingshot's house. "You know what I think? I think you read too many comic books."

"You have a better explanation?" Stump asked.

I had to admit, I did not. I didn't have a worse one, either. I didn't have any explanation at all.

"I think he should lay off the forkball," I said.

# ★ CHAPTER 9 ★

**W**e found Slingshot kneeling on his black-
top driveway, well away from the garage.
At first I thought he must've been praying to the
gods of baseball, asking them to give him back
his fastball.

Then I saw the rocket.

It was a flaming orange, streamlined
beauty. From its winged base to the tip of its
bulging silver nose cone, it stood at least three
feet tall.

"Steady, boys," Slingshot warned as we rode
closer. "This thing is packed to the gills with
gunpowder."

"For real?" asked Velcro, his eyes widening

as he slowed down and steered clear of the rocket.

"Yep," said Slingshot, rising and backing away from the rocket. "I'm working on an experiment. You're just in time." He held a black battery pack in his hands. Thin wires ran from the pack to the three-legged launchpad on which the rocket stood. In the middle of the battery pack was a red ignition button. Slingshot's thumb hovered over it.

We dumped our bikes near the garage, then ran back for a closer look at the contraption. Tall and slender, the rocket was topped with an egg-shaped nose. The long body appeared to be made of cardboard, kind of like an extra-long paper towel tube. Three balsa wood fins, painted white, encircled the base like the flights of an arrow.

"Did you make it?" I asked.

"The body and payload, I did," Slingshot said. "The engines I got from the Toy Box, downtown."

"What's that big bump at the top?" Stump asked. "I thought rockets were supposed to be sleek."

"That's the payload," Slingshot explained. "When the rocket reaches the peak of its flight, the nose cone will spring open and deliver a load of cargo."

"Will it really fly?" I asked.

"Fly?" Slingshot snorted. "Man, this baby will soar like the space shuttle. I gave her three separate booster packs. Each one carries a big charge of powder—high-octane model-rocket fuel. According to my calculations, she should reach a top altitude of about three thousand feet."

"Three thousand feet!" I exclaimed. "That's more than half a mile!"

"Just over," agreed Slingshot. ".568 miles, to be precise."

"Higher than the Empire State Building!" Velcro said.

"Higher than any building in the world," said Slingshot.

"Sky high," said Stump.

"That's the idea." Slingshot nodded. "You guys ever hear of something called cloud seeding?"

We shook our heads. I'd heard of cloud computing (though I wasn't sure what it was) and play-off seeding (which I understood well). But I'd never heard of cloud seeding.

"Cloud seeding," said Slingshot, "is something scientists do to try to make it rain. Basically they use rockets to shoot certain chemicals, like dry ice, into clouds. The idea is that the chemicals will cause water particles in the clouds to freeze into ice. If the ice chunks get heavy enough, they fall as snow or rain."

"That's whack," Velcro said. "No one can make rain."

Stump shot him a look. Clearly he thought at least one person could.

"Cloud seeding is real," Slingshot said. "Lots of countries with drought problems do it. A guy named Vincent Schaefer came up with it like fifty years ago. He was a chemist. Google it if you don't believe me."

I didn't have to look it up. Like I've said, Slingshot is a science whiz. Nutty as it sounded, if he said cloud seeding was real, I believed him.

I only had one question.

"Why do you want it to rain?" I asked. "I kind of think we've had enough rain around here."

"I don't," said Slingshot.

Now I was really confused.

"But I thought you just said . . ."

"What I said is that cloud seeding is a way of changing the weather. I've been thinking, if you can use rockets to make rain, why not use them to stop rain?" He paused and looked closely at us. "Maybe you've noticed that every time I pitch lately, it starts pouring?"

We shifted our feet uncomfortably, glanced away. Yeah, we'd noticed, all right.

"Kind of hard to miss," Slingshot said. "Anyway, I've packed the payload with stuff that makes water disappear. This is a cloud *un*seeding rocket. It's designed to make rain go away."

I looked up at the sky. A few fluffy white clouds drifted high overhead. They didn't look particularly threatening. If you squinted, a long, lumpy one sort of looked like a dragon, but not a very fierce dragon.

A real dragon would've been nice. They breathe fire. A jet of flaming dragon breath would probably dry out the air better than any homemade rocket.

"What kind of stuff did you put in the rocket?" I asked.

"You ever see those little white packets that sometimes come in the box when you buy something electronic? Like if your parents get a new camera or phone? They usually say WARNING: DO NOT EAT! on them."

"Why would anyone eat a little white plastic packet from inside a camera box?" Velcro wondered.

"Beats me," said Slingshot. "Anyway, those packets contain a mineral called silica. It's like tiny grains of ground-up stone. Silica absorbs moisture. They put those little packets in boxes—computers, cameras, furniture, even shoes and clothes—to keep mold from growing while the stuff is being shipped from the factory. Moisture in the air causes mold. Silica dries out the air."

"Got it," I said. "So you collected a bunch of these silica packets and emptied them into the rocket. Cool idea."

"Not exactly," Slingshot said. "I couldn't find enough of them to get as much silica as I needed. It's not like my parents are always going out and buying new electronics. Fortunately, there is one common household item that has tons of the stuff in it." He paused. He didn't look like he wanted to say more.

"So tell us," I urged him. "What's your secret ingredient?"

Slingshot sighed. "Kitty litter," he said.

"Kitty litter is packed with silica . . . for obvious reasons."

"Kitty litter!" shouted Velcro. "You're going to blast the sky with kitty litter?"

Mr. Bones cocked his head. I swear he was following our conversation. The way he panted made it look like he was laughing. *Silly cats,* you could almost hear him thinking. *You'll never catch me pooping in a box. Gross!*

"What?" said Slingshot. "It came straight out of a fresh bag. It's clean. And it works. Kitty litter definitely soaks up, well, you know . . . wetness."

"Enough talk!" said Stump. "When do we launch this bad boy?"

"How about now?" said Slingshot, relieved to change the subject.

I have to say, Slingshot is awesome at inventing things. He once designed a pair of sandpaper golf spikes to help Velcro stop slipping on a frozen outfield. Another time he cooked up a magic potion that, he convinced the Rounders, would make my terrible hitting slump go away. It was a horrible potion, full of foot powder and pepper flakes. I didn't want to, but I finally drank the rotten stuff. And the very next day, what do you know? I hit a homer off Flicker Pringle to win the championship.

But a three-stage model rocket packed full of kitty litter to stop rain that hadn't even started yet? That was something new. If you asked me, Slingshot was pushing the limit.

Right now, however, he was about to push something else: the red button on the engine igniter.

"Everybody move back," he commanded as he unspooled the wire.

"You too, Mr. Bones," I said. I grabbed my dog by the collar, and we all took about twenty big steps away from the rocket.

"Will it be loud?" asked Velcro, covering his ears.

"Gosh, I hope so," said Stump.

"Should be more of a *whoosh* than a bang,"

Slingshot answered. Then he began the count-down.

We all joined in:

"Ten . . . nine . . . eight . . . seven . . . six . . . five . . . four . . . three . . . two . . . one . . . LIFT-OFF!"

Slingshot pressed the red button. A split second later, flames shot out the back of the rocket. Then, with a mighty *FOOMPH*, it shot into the sky, trailing a streak of flame and smoke. Moving faster than anything I'd ever seen, it pierced the fluffy clouds like an arrow. A second later, the rocket disappeared from view altogether. As we shielded our eyes and scanned the sky to see where it went, we heard a faint *pop* from high overhead and began to cheer. The sound could mean only one thing: The nose cone had sprung open and was seeding the sky with kitty litter.

"That was awesome!" Stump shouted.

A moment later, the rocket reappeared. Dangling from a big red parachute, it drifted slowly back to earth. It was a beautiful sight. We raced to get under it. Before it touched down, a shower of grit began falling from the sky. It bounced on the driveway and grass like dancing fleas.

"Ouch," I said as stinging bits landed on my head. "What have you done, Slingshot?"

Then it dawned on me. Kitty litter. It was raining kitty litter.

Slingshot retrieved the rocket. "Okay," he said with a look of determination as the sand shower let up. "Now we test my hypothesis. Grab your mitts."

He put on his own and prepared to fire a pitch. "If the experiment worked, it won't rain."

I pulled my own glove off the handlebars of my bike and settled into a crouch to give Slingshot a target. "C'mon, baby, hum it in here," I urged.

My friend wound up just as he would in a game. He kicked and let the pitch fly. Before the ball left his hand, I felt a shadow cross my body.

Then I felt the first sprinkles.

Slingshot's face fell. But it did not fall nearly as hard as the rain. Huge drops exploded on the ground like water balloons as I caught the pitch and beat a hasty retreat toward the house.

"Houston," I shouted over the downpour as I ran, "we have a problem!"

We all dodged into the house. Slingshot's mom and dad invited us to stay for lunch. I accepted. They served grilled eggplant.

Things were going from bad to worse.

# ★ CHAPTER 10 ★

**W**ord of Slingshot's troubles reached Windsor before our team bus did. When we arrived to take on the Gaskets, a huge playoff crowd was ready for us. Even though there wasn't a cloud in the sky, lots of people wore raincoats and carried umbrellas.

Many of them also carried signs.

No Rain, No Gain! read one.

Pitcher, Pitcher, Go Away, the Windsor Gaskets Want to Play said another.

"Ignore them," I told Slingshot as we loosened up before the game. "They don't know anything."

Easier said than done. The fans were loud, and some of the signs they waved were the size of tarps. Real tarps would have been nice. We could have used them to cover the diamond in case it really did start to rain.

Slingshot gulped nervously. He took the ball, but instead of throwing any practice pitches, he just stood on the sidelines rubbing the old pill in his hands. I could tell he was worried about unleashing a storm.

Skip Lou watched him closely. After a few seconds, he quietly called Gilly over and told him to loosen his arm, just in case we needed him to pitch.

"BATTER UP!" roared the ump.

Ducks Bunion pulled on a helmet and strode up to the plate. The Windsor pitcher fed him a fastball. Ducks swung right through it.

"STEE-RIKE ONE!" barked the ump.

Dervish Luft tossed the ball back to the mound. The pitcher wound up and threw another fastball. This time Ducks was on it like green on grass. He ripped a line-drive single to left field.

Stump came up next and flew out to right.

With one out and one on, it was my turn to hit. I grabbed my favorite Louisville Slugger from Billy Wishes and rubbed the batboy's head for luck.

"Go get 'em, Walloper," he said.

I sure meant to try. I was mad at those fans. I wanted to make them pay for razzing Slingshot. At the very least, I wanted to make them be quiet.

The pitcher started me with a fastball on the inside corner. I let it go for strike one. I was looking for something waist high and down the middle. He threw an outside changeup and a high fastball for balls one and two. Then he served up the pitch I wanted. A big, lazy meatball that floated over the fat part of the plate.

I pounced. My swing came free and easy. The ball thundered into the sky. The minute it left my bat, I knew it was gone.

I put my head down and galloped around the bases, enjoying the silence that settled over the ballpark as the ball landed in the centerfield bleachers. It got so quiet so fast, you would have sworn someone had hit a mute button somewhere. A well-timed dinger will do that to a hostile crowd.

Tugboat came up after me and grounded to short for our second out. Gasser followed him and popped to the third baseman in foul territory to end the top half of the inning.

Leading 2–0, we grabbed our gloves and took our positions in the field.

The minute Slingshot stepped onto the mound, the ballpark started buzzing again. Wise guys in the stands opened their umbrellas. A heckler in the first-base seats stopped chewing his hot dog long enough to shout, "Hey, kid, what're you doing after the game? My lawn needs watering!"

At that, Skip Lou charged from the bench and collared the ump behind home plate. I'd never seen him so hot. If he were an egg, he would have been fried. A real egg would have been nice. I would have pasted that obnoxious heckler with it.

The ump nodded vigorously and strode over to the sideline, where he warned the fans to knock off the insults.

Throughout the delay, I kept my eyes on Slingshot. His head hung low. His shoulders slumped like he was carrying a sack of anvils. Maybe Stump was right. Maybe Slingshot was sending off such plumes of negative energy that his mood actually affected the weather. There was no way to know for sure. All I could say with certainty was that my friend looked like he'd rather be anywhere else in the world than standing on a pitcher's mound with the ball in his hand.

My heart flip-flopped in my chest. I knew exactly how he felt. When I was stuck in the worst hitting slump in history, just the thought of trying to hit made me dizzy. It got so bad I wanted to make like my swing and disappear.

"Concentrate, Slingshot," I called. "You can do it!" I crouched down in ready position, crossed the fingers on my throwing hand, and began visualizing images of dry things. I thought of towels, sand dunes, chapped lips, kitty litter.

The ump settled in behind Tugboat.

"BATTER UP!" he bellowed.

The Gasket leadoff hitter tapped the plate with his bat and waited for the first pitch. I sent a mental image of saltine crackers Slingshot's way.

The pitcher started his windup. As he brought his hands together over his head, a low rumble rippled through the ballpark. Slingshot didn't wait for what he knew was coming. He didn't throw the pitch, either. He just ducked his head and sprinted off the mound before his pitching could unleash the deluge that would drown us all. So much for saltines.

"Time out!" called Skip Lou.

The ump beat him to it. He took one look at the darkening sky and ordered us all off the field.

"There may be lightning in the area," he explained.

We raced off the diamond and into the dugout, where Slingshot sat at the end of the bench with his head in his hands. Mr. Bones bounded over and licked his face. He's a friendly dog and very good at sensing moods. As far as he's concerned, his job in life is to cheer people up. It's about the only thing he takes seriously.

Slingshot raised his head and scratched Mr. Bones behind the ears.

"Sorry, guys," the pitcher mumbled, "I didn't mean to let you down again."

"You're not letting us down," I said. "The weather is."

"Every time I pitch, it rains. It's all my fault."

"No way," said the Glove. "It rains every time I play second base, too. That doesn't mean I'm causing the rain. Think about it. We've just been having some freaky weather, is all."

Every player on the team roundly backed up the Glove.

"Crazy," Gilly said.

"Bad luck," said Tugboat.

"Nothing to it," agreed Ocho.

Stump, Velcro, and I traded glances. Now probably would not be a good time to spill the beans about Slingshot's rocket experiment. Keeping our information to ourselves, we joined the general chorus of support. But Slingshot wasn't buying what we were selling. He insisted the nutty showers were more than pure coincidence. He claimed they amounted to a pattern. Nothing we said could change his mind.

"I'm not going back in," he said, his voice breaking like a curveball. It dropped so low we could barely hear him. "This is playoff baseball. It's win or go home. And the only way to win is to play. In other words, we don't want a rainout." He buried his head in his hands again.

With Slingshot shelved, Skip Lou needed to jigger the lineup. And he needed to do it fast. The sky already was clearing, and the record crowd was starting to get antsy. Skip grabbed his clipboard and studied the roster. After scratching out a few different combinations in pencil, he hit upon one that gave us a decent chance of salvaging the game.

"Listen up, guys," he announced. "Here's what we're going to do. Gilly, I'm moving you from first base to pitcher. Kid Rabbit, you take over at first. Velcro will stay on the bench for now, but after three innings he'll go to center field and Gasser will relieve Gilly on the mound."

By the time Skip finished making his changes, the sun shone once more.

"PLAY BALL!" called the umpire.

The Windsor fans closed their umbrellas and cheered loudly.

Minus Slingshot, the Rounders returned to the field. Our pitcher stayed on the bench with Mr. Bones's head in his lap and a faraway look in his eyes.

Gilly fired a few warm-up pitches to Tugboat, then the batter stepped into the box and the game started back up. I have to admit, I don't remember much about it. I was too distracted by worrying about Slingshot to think clearly. I know the innings passed quickly. In the third, Dervish homered with a man aboard to tie the score at two. An inning later, we strung together a bunch of hits and slipped in front again by a single run.

The game reached the bottom of the sixth with the score still 3–2 in our favor. By then Gasser, who relieved Gilly at the start of the fourth, was tiring. He walked the leadoff batter to put the tying run aboard with no outs. The next guy hit a fly ball to Ducks, allowing the runner to tag up and take second base. The third Gasket batter sizzled a grounder to the Glove, who threw to Kid Rabbit for the out at first. Once again, the runner advanced. With two down, he stood on my base. The tying run was only sixty feet away.

"C'mon now, Gasser," I shouted. "One more. You can do it!"

The Windsor center fielder stepped up to

the plate, a tall, lanky kid with a lot of pop in his swing.

I glanced over at our dugout. Slingshot had straightened up on the bench and was following the action intently. He caught my eye and suddenly waved for me to come over.

"Now?" I mouthed.

He nodded vigorously.

I called time and ran to find out what was on Slingshot's mind.

"This guy can hit a ton," my friend whispered. "Anything in his wheelhouse you can kiss good-bye."

"How should Gasser pitch him?"

"Fastballs low and away," Slingshot said. "Don't give him anything else. Definitely don't give him anything over the plate."

I thanked him for the scouting report and relayed his advice to Gasser.

The Windsor fence buster dug in once again. The runner on third inched off the bag. Gasser wound up and fired his pitch. As soon as he let go, he shook his head. He knew right away he'd missed his spot.

Like a homing pigeon returning to its roost, the ball never wavered in its flight. It zipped straight from Gasser's hand toward the heart of the strike zone. The batter swung viciously. The ball changed direction so fast that I practically got whiplash jerking around to watch it sail high and deep.

The ball was still in the air when the guy on third crossed the plate with the tying run. It still soared as the batter who clobbered it rounded second and bore down on me. It flew all the way to the fence in deepest center field and seemed destined to clear it.

Only one thing stood between us and playoff elimination.

Velcro Ramirez.

And Velcro wasn't exactly standing.

He was jumping into the air like a jack in the box on a pogo stick.

Timing his leap perfectly, Velcro speared

the ball just as it left the yard.

On the bench, Slingshot and Mr. Bones slapped high fives.

The batter was out. The run didn't count.

Final score: Rounders 3, Gaskets 2.

We had done it. With a pair of gutsy substitute pitching performances and one heroic leap, we had won the game and forced a championship showdown with the Haymakers.

Once again, everything would be on the line.

Exactly the way we had always dreamed it would be.

Now we just needed to cure Slingshot of his pitching blues. I hoped a few days of rafting, far from any baseball diamond, would do the trick.

# ★ CHAPTER 11 ★

Early Friday morning, a caravan of cars pulled away from our house. The sun was still low in the sky, and mist rose from warming front lawns as we wound down the street like a big mechanical snake. It looked like it was going to be a nice dry day. I knew for a fact it would be a great one. We were finally on our way to the North Woods.

There were six cars altogether, each one packed to the gills with kids and camping gear. I sat in the middle row of the lead minivan, with Stump to my right and Slingshot on my left. Mr. Bones shared the back with our tents and the rest of our gear. My dad drove, and Stump's dad rode shotgun. Before we even reached the high-way, we'd already tortured them with eighteen choruses of "Ninety-Nine Bottles of Root Beer on the Wall."

"Forget root beer. What I could use is a coffee," Dad said to Mr. Plumwhiff, rubbing sleep from his eyes.

"I'd settle for earplugs," Mr. Plumwhiff replied as we launched into the next verse of the world's longest song. He swiveled in his seat to face us. "Are you boys planning to sing the whole way?"

"Eighty-one bottles of root beer on the wall, eighty one bottles of root beer," we belted by way of an answer. "If one of those bottles should happen to fall, eighty bottles of root beer on the wall!"

Mr. Bones barked along happily to the words.

"This could make for a long drive," my dad muttered.

"It feels like an eternity already," said Mr. Plumwhiff.

In fact, the trip lasted only about two hours. We sang for less than half of it. The rest of the time, we played yellow-car skittles.

Whenever someone saw a yellow car, he shouted, "Skittles!" Whoever said it first got a point. If two people yelled at the same time, you could jinx the other guy. Then he couldn't talk until someone said his name. That was the best, because then you could nab more points.

I got on the board first and led Stump and Slingshot by a score of two to one when Stump jinxed me on a Mini Cooper. Rats! I should have been quicker!

Knocked from the game, there was nothing much to do except look out the window. As the van speeded ahead, I watched the woods grow deeper and the towns fewer and smaller the farther north we got. After a while, there seemed to be no towns at all, only the occasional white farmhouse with a big stack of firewood on the porch.

A few minutes after jinxing me, Stump nailed

Slingshot on a fast, jet-plane-loud Camaro. Suddenly our own car got awfully quiet.

"That's more like it," said Stump's dad. "Peace at last."

Stump didn't like that, so he said my name and then I unjinxed Slingshot.

We passed a shingled cabin, its dirt yard littered with rusted tractors. Hanging from its mailbox was a sign offering live bait for sale.

"What kind of bait, do you think?" I asked.

"Night crawlers, probably," Dad said. "They would grow nice and fat in this farm soil. Trout must love 'em."

"Padiddle!" blurted Stump, socking me on my shoulder.

"Ow," I cried. "Who said anything about padiddle?"

"Padiddle!" yelled Slingshot in answer. "Ohio." He socked my other shoulder.

I forgot about night crawlers and started scanning the road for out-of-state license plates.

The game of padiddle is pretty much like

"punch buggy," except you're looking for cars with out-of-state license plates instead of Volkswagen Beetles. They can be any color. You see one, you shout, "Padiddle!" and thump the other guys. It's kind of ridiculous, but that didn't stop us. Pretty soon the middle seat looked like a boxing match for snails, if snails had boxing matches: It was a real slugfest.

Not that we really drilled each other. Our punches were just hard enough to let the other guys know they'd been beaten. The trouble was, there were a lot of them. Abenaki Park reaches into three different states and draws tourists from all over the country. Plus, I was riding in the middle, so I got hammered from both sides.

"That was a bus!" Stump complained as I paid him for missing a Greyhound with New York tags.

"Sure is," I agreed. Buses definitely count. So do motorcycles. Anything with a motor that moves, we count.

"Padiddle!" cried Slingshot as a station wagon with Montana plates passed us on the left and Mr. Bones yapped excitedly.

"That should count double," Stump suggested with a grin. "Montana's so far away."

Easy for him to say. He wasn't sitting next to Slingshot.

"One's plenty," I said, stiffening my shoulder.

We were still playing half an hour later when Dad turned off the main road and onto a narrow track that wound alongside a fast-running river. The Big Fork! A few minutes later a broad wooden sign with yellow letters officially welcomed us to the park. Pine trees towered above the road on all sides, casting a net of shadows.

A real net would have been nice. We could have used it to catch some of the trout swimming in the river.

Dad eased up next to a log ranger station and, following directions taped in the window, tapped the car horn. The hut's screen door slapped open, and a ranger ambled down the wooden steps. He wore mirrored sunglasses, hiking boots, and a Smokey the Bear–style hat.

I rolled down my window and a rich, woodsy smell of pine instantly filled the car.

"Wow," said Slingshot. "Some of those giants must be two hundred years old or more."

"Oh, man!" said Stump. "Can we get out here? Please?"

Mr. Bones seconded the idea with a couple eager barks. The ranger leaned against the driver's door and handed Dad a park pass through the window. "Camping?" he asked.

"Camping and rafting," Dad told him. "Us, and the five cars behind us."

"Rafting, huh? You made arrangements for the cars?"

"Sure did," said Dad. "We'll get on the rafts at Six Mile Cove, and the guys up there will drive our cars back here for us. They tell me they'll be waiting for us when we come off the river tomorrow."

"Perfect," said the ranger. "Well, you sure picked a good time. With all this fluky rain, the Big Fork is really ripping. Hear it? You're in for the ride of your lives." He turned and winked at the guys and me.

I listened carefully. Sure enough, from through the trees came the sound of rushing water, music far sweeter than "Ninety-Nine Bottles of Root Beer" ever could hope to be.

"You've been getting these showers, too?" Dad asked, handing over the park fee for all six cars. "None in the weekend forecast, I hope."

"Not at the moment," the ranger replied. "But that's what's been so strange. One minute the sun will be shining, then out of nowhere it'll cloud up and we'll get a real gullywasher. Strange summer."

"Same back home," Dad said.

I nudged Slingshot.

"Hear that?" I whispered. "Freak showers."

"Yeah," agreed Stump. "So unless you've been sneaking up here to pitch, I'd say they have nothing to do with you."

"Exactly!" I said.

Slingshot said nothing, just ducked his head as if avoiding a dodgeball.

"Well, keep your fingers crossed the worst is past," continued the ranger. "Other than that, have a great time! I'll look for you tomorrow afternoon." He touched his fingers to his hat and turned to amble back into his hut.

We went deeper into the forest for another half hour, the other five cars humping along behind us like the world's biggest inchworm. Every few minutes, the trees cleared and we caught a glimpse of the river. Mr. Bones did a little dance each time it came into view. I knew how he felt. I was bursting to ditch the car and get onto the water myself. Somewhere along that river, I knew, lay the Devil's Furnace. I couldn't wait to see the legendary place. And maybe, if we were lucky, find the lost treasure.

"Are you sure you're up for it, Mr. Bones?" I asked with a laugh. "Remember that puddle back by the willow tree after the Lumleyville rainout? It swallowed you whole!"

"Oh, man," said Stump. "Mr. Bones sank like a stone. That thing was a lake."

"You better wear a life vest for this trip, old boy," said Slingshot. "We can't risk losing our mascot!"

"We're all going to wear life vests," said Mr. Plumwhiff, turning in his seat. "Helmets, too. It's a rafting rule. Plus, it's just common sense."

"Even Mr. Bones?" I asked.

"Vest, yes," said Dad. "We have a special one for him. I think he can get by without a helmet."

"Your head's plenty hard, right, pal?" I laughed.

Mr. Bones lunged forward over the seat and licked my face. His tail paddled the air like an oar.

When I looked up, we were sliding into the gravel parking lot of a rustic wooden lodge on the banks of the Big Fork River. Dad snapped off the engine, and we leaped from our seats just as the rest of the caravan nosed into parking spots.

We had arrived!

# ★ CHAPTER 12 ★

"This place is awesome!" gushed Ocho as he ran up, rubbing his shoulder. The rest of the guys followed on his heels.

"Padiddle?" I asked.

"Middle padiddle," he said. "I got it from both sides."

"Tell me about it," I said.

"Let's check out the lodge," suggested Tugboat.

I glanced across the parking area. The dark brown building looked really cool, like the sort of place where Daniel Boone might've hung his coonskin cap between expeditions. It was wide and tall, with a deep porch and a massive stone chimney rising from the wood-shingled roof. A gravel path led down to the river behind it, where a flotilla of rafts bobbed at the docks.

"Can we explore?" I called to my dad.

"Sure," he answered. "But just for a minute or two. Don't go far."

We dashed across the lot and bounded onto the porch of the lodge. It was furnished with benches made of rough planks laid across varnished tree stumps.

"Sweet," said the Glove, taking a seat.

"Made from white pine harvested right here in the park," boomed a voice from above. It sounded like rolling thunder.

We looked around.

"Up here," said the voice. "Hand me that last lightbulb, will you?"

The man stood atop a ladder with his head in the porch rafters.

Billy grabbed a lightbulb from a toolbox on the floor and handed it up to him.

"Thanks," grunted the man, who was

dressed like a ranger. "We're changing over to high-efficiency bulbs. Use about ninety percent less energy than the old ones." He screwed the bulb into a hanging fixture made out of deer antlers. "There. Done." He climbed down. "Joe Wood," he said, extending his hand. "Park guide and all-around handyman."

I shook his hand. I winced. It crushed like a vise.

"We're going rafting," Billy told him.

"Are you now?" asked Joe Wood, smiling.

"Yessir!" said Billy. "We're a baseball team. Only we don't have any games for a few days, so the whole team is celebrating by going rafting. Camping and rafting."

"Wait a minute," said Joe Wood. "Back up. You're a baseball team, but you're celebrating not playing any games? What am I missing?"

"Actually, it's our final season as a team. What we're really celebrating is all our years together," Tugboat explained.

"Oh, now I get it," said the man. "A last-stand

kind of deal." He turned to Billy.

"Exactly," agreed Billy. "Is your name really Joe Wood? You're a forest ranger named Wood?"

I groaned. Leave it to Billy. The guy was going to think we were real dorks.

"Yeah," chimed in Stump. "That's like a teacher being named Lesson or something. But Wood is cooler. There was a great pitcher named Joe Wood."

In spite of myself, I nodded.

Surprisingly, so did the guide. He also broke into a grin. Which was a big relief.

"Howard Ellsworth 'Smoky Joe' Wood," he said. "One of the all-time greats. Pitched Boston to the 1912 World Series title. Went thirty-four and five that year, with an ERA of one point nine one and two hundred fifty-eight strikeouts."

Stump's mouth popped open like a suitcase with a busted hinge. All of ours did. The guy knew baseball!

Joe Wood winked.

Just then Mr. Bones flew across the grass

in a blur and hurled himself at our new friend. Now it was Joe Wood's turn to be surprised.

"Down, boy!" I called as my dog leaped upon the guide, tongue first. First Billy grills the guy, then Mr. Bones marinates him. This was getting seriously embarrassing. "I'm sorry," I said. "He's really friendly. He always seems to know when people like dogs. Uh, you do like dogs, don't you?"

"Who do we have here?" Joe Wood asked, scooping up Mr. Bones and rocking him in his arms like a baby.

Mr. Bones swooned. He lay perfectly still, his big brown eyes fixed adoringly on the guide's smooth face.

"Like 'em? I love them." Joe Wood laughed. "Isn't this whole region the native home of the Abenaki Indians? Well, did you know the Abenaki loved dogs? Treated them like members of the family. They have all kinds of stories about dogs. Real dog people. How could I work here and not love man's best friend?"

*Whew,* I thought. I was glad the Abenaki weren't cat people. That could have been awkward.

"Mr. Bones definitely is a member of our family," said Ocho. "The Rounders wouldn't be complete without him. If only he could swing a bat, we'd send him up to hit."

Mr. Bones wagged like a pine bough in a gale.

"He sure swings his tail pretty well." Joe Wood laughed. He set my dog back on the ground. "So you guys are rafting. How far do you plan to go?"

"All the way," I said.

The guide's expression turned serious.

"Ever hear of a place called the Devil's Furnace?" he asked.

"You bet we have," gushed Billy. "We've heard about the treasure, too!"

"Is there any truth to the legend?" I asked.

"Good question," said the guide. "Let me put it this way. I've been searching for that cavern ever since I was a kid, and I've never found it. But, wow, if those old stories hold any truth at all, just think what might be hidden in the cave. Assuming it actually exists, of course."

"Gold," said Stump. "Gold and a pile of animal furs, that's what!"

"Any of you fellows know anything about dowsing?" Joe Wood suddenly asked.

"You mean getting soaked?" I asked, thinking of Slingshot's last few pitching efforts. "Yeah, we know too much."

"I mean using a forked stick to find stuff," said the guide. He stepped off the porch. "Follow me and I'll show you."

He walked over to a willow tree at the corner of the lodge and snapped off a Y-shaped branch.

"Dowsing is an ancient way of discovering groundwater. What you do is, you hold the two forked ends of a willow branch in your hands like this and slowly pace back and forth over a likely spot. It's got to be a willow branch. Some people say hazel works, too, but true believers claim willow's best. When the dowsing rod senses water, it starts to twitch."

"Like a metal detector," said Ocho.

"Without the batteries," said Joe Wood.

"Seriously?" asked Velcro. "A stick can lead you to water? No offense, but it sounds kind of kooky."

The guide winked. "Some people call it water witching," he said. "Believe it or not, there are folks around here who swear by it. They bring in a professional dowser when they need to dig a new well." He paused. "The thing is, dowsers will tell you water witching works with things other than water. Buried metals and gemstones, for example."

"Gold!" shouted Stump.

"Gold," agreed the guide. "I've always thought the trick would be to paddle into the Devil's Furnace during a heavy rain, when the whirlpool is swirling. Your timing would have to be perfect, because the old Big Fork is cunning. It has as many secrets as it does bends, eddies, back currents, rips, and rapids."

"Of course, you know the Highway Bandit stuff is all just legend." He winked again. "Like I said, I've searched high and low for the cavern and never found a thing."

We pressed him for more information, but he just shrugged. "Fellas," he said, handing the willow branch to Slingshot, I wish I could stay and chat, but I've got to get back to work. My advice: Listen to the river. If it really does have a secret, maybe it'll whisper something to you. That, and watch out for the rapids at the Devil's Furnace. They are one hundred percent real."

With that he turned and strode into the lodge. For our own part, we headed back across the parking lot. Our dads were calling. We had some gear to unload.

About nineteen tons of it.

Working quickly, we got our stuff out of the cars and humped over to the lodge like a pack of camels.

"I'll tell you what," Dad said once everything was stacked on the porch. "You kids kick back here, and we'll go and make sure the rafts are ready." He and the rest of the dads disappeared behind the lodge.

We stretched out to wait. Rolled-up sleeping bags turn out to make comfortable seats.

"When's lunch?" asked Tugboat as soon as we were settled. "I'm starving."

My stomach rumbled in agreement. Nothing like pulling a Sherpa to work up an appetite. I tugged open my backpack and pulled out a bag of homemade gorp: good old raisins and peanuts. A camping classic. My own recipe also included M&M's and granola.

Soon we were all munching away. Mr. Bones stared longingly.

"Sorry, old pal," I said. "No gorp for you. It has chocolate in it. Not to mention, peanuts make you fart."

"Gross," said Gasser. "He's not staying in my tent, that's for sure. No offense, Mr. B."

"You should talk," said Gilly. "You're the one named Gasser!"

"Yeah, and you're the guy who stunk up the whole dorm at baseball camp last summer!"

While the guys razzed each other, I found Mr. Bones's bowl and filled it with dry dog food from a bag.

He shot me a dirty look, like, "Years of blind love and this is how you repay me? With jaw-breaking little nuggets of who knows what? I mean, would you eat this stuff?"

"I know, I know," I apologized, giving him a pat. "Not exactly five star. But just wait until we hit the campsite this afternoon. Hot dogs and hamburgers galore!"

His ears perked right up and he managed a wag or two.

Shortly afterward, our dads returned. They took one look at us and shook their heads.

"I hope you saved some for later," Tugboat's dad said. "No grocery stores on the river, you know."

"We were starving," said Tugboat. "Plus, you guys took forever."

"More like ten minutes," said Mr. Tooley. "But who's counting? In any case, we're all set. Three rafts ready to go. Now pass me a couple sandwiches. I could eat a moose."

We finished lunch and headed down to the boats. Three dockhands met us and showed us the ropes. They were high school kids with summer jobs at the park. Wrangling rafts by the river with friends all day looked like pretty cool work. I decided on the spot to add dockhand to the list of things I'd like to be when I grew up, right after Major League ballplayer and spy.

Each of the inflatable boats had room for six paddlers. Slingshot, Stump, Velcro, Mr. Plumwhiff, my dad, and I, along with Mr. Bones, would take the last of the three in our river train. The teenagers lent a hand loading our stuff, shifting bags and coolers around to balance the weight. They produced a long rubber sack and told us we should put any valuables we didn't want to get wet inside of it. Wallets, cameras, phones, and stuff like that.

"Because you will get wet," they said. "Especially if you plan to run the Devil's Furnace!"

With the cargo properly stowed, the workers helped strap on our life vests and red plastic helmets. Then they handed each of us a paddle, and we climbed aboard. Mr. Bones commandeered a post in the bow, his tail wagging like a signal flag. The rest of us perched right up on our bulging raft's pontoonlike rubber sides, balancing a foot or so above the rippling water.

One at a time, the rafts in front of us shoved off, and we cheered them on their way.

Then it was our turn.

At my dad's command, we pushed into the current. The river nudged us gently forward, and away we bobbed like an overfed petting-zoo duck. As we approached the first bend, I sneaked a quick backward glance at the lodge. Even as it disappeared from view, something told me we'd be seeing more of Joe Wood before our adventure ended. He had seemed to know more about the legend of the Devil's Furnace than he had let on. I think he kind of wanted us to believe the legend, just as he had when he was a kid. I knew for a fact the guys wouldn't miss an opportunity to search for the treasure. If we somehow got lucky, I felt sure Joe Wood would be the first in line to congratulate us.

I turned and dipped my paddle. The raft quivered beneath me like the floor of a bounce house. The river sang its merry tune.

# ★ CHAPTER 13 ★

The Big Fork flowed wide and flat, studded here and there with slick gray boulders. Its banks were rocky and moss covered, crowded with overhanging trees. Under the water, the pebbly bottom flashed by, as colorful as a mosaic.

"This is the life," crowed Dad as we drifted downstream about a strong relay throw behind the other rafts. The soft current did most of the work. We used our paddles only occasionally, to sweep around curves.

"You said it," agreed Stump's dad. "Who's up for some bug juice?"

I don't know if he was actually thirsty or just

couldn't resist mentioning bug juice. Stump, Slingshot, and I raised our paddles in the air, and Mr. Plumwhiff flipped the lid off the cooler and pulled out a jug of fruit punch.

"Drink up, me hearties," he growled like a pirate as he filled three plastic cups. "Later on we won't have time. We'll be busy paddling."

The punch was sweet and good. It didn't taste anything like bugs. Not that I've ever eaten bugs. Maybe the occasional gnat has flown into my mouth or something, but I don't make a habit of it.

We rounded a big turn where the woods briefly opened on a wide green meadow, birds flitting between tall tufts of grass. I could imagine deer and moose gathering there to drink from the cool river, picture long-ago native hunting parties stealthily tracking them.

"Must be Elk Bend," said Slingshot, consulting a waterproof map. "Cool."

After gliding past the meadow, the river suddenly quickened. The water deepened, darkening to a piney green as it funneled between steep granite ledges. The rock walls blotted out the sun, and the air temperature seemed to plunge by thirty degrees.

"Hold on now," warned Dad. "We're going to pick up some speed."

He wasn't kidding. All of a sudden, the river turned into a roller coaster. As we surged ahead, my stomach leaped like a salmon. I grabbed the handles on the side of the raft and held on for dear life. My efforts may have kept me in the boat, but they did nothing to block the shrill screeching sound that suddenly began to bounce off the river's high banks.

"Are they singing?" Stump asked, stretching to see what the guys in the rafts ahead of us were up to.

"Wailing, more like," I said, my neck hairs prickling at the eerie noise. It sounded like a haunted teakettle.

A real kettle would have been nice. We could've used it to make something warm to drink. At the bottom of the deeply shaded canyon, in the wind, I suddenly felt colder than a penguin with the sniffles.

Mr. Bones pricked up his ears and started howling.

"Easy, boy, it's nothing," I said.

Using his paddle like a beaver uses its tail, Stump slapped the frothing water. "Cut that out!" he hollered. "You're upsetting Mr. Bones!"

The wailing increased in volume and pitch. Stump paddle-slapped the water angrily, sure he was being made fun of.

Big mistake.

His karate chops tossed our raft off balance, and we spun into a sharp one-eighty. Mr. Bones was flung backward from the bow and landed in the bottom of the raft. He bounced up, barking.

Then next thing I knew, we were hurtling backward down the Big Fork.

"Who put this crazy thing in reverse?" asked Mr. Plumwhiff as his cup went flying and punch sloshed all over his T-shirt. Bug juice tie-dye, it looked like.

I craned my head around and gasped at what I saw.

"Uh, guys?" I said.

We were plowing straight for a jagged rock wall.

Fast.

A real plow would have been nice. Those things are built like tanks and would survive a collision. Our rubber raft would not. The rocks looked like giant teeth. They would chew us up like a piece of Dubble Bubble.

The others saw the danger at the same moment I did.

"Port side," barked Dad. "Paddle! Hard!"

"English?" I shouted over the horrible whistling.

"Left!" shouted Dad. "Left side of the raft, paddle! Now!"

Slingshot and I dug in with all our might.

The boat didn't turn. The wall jumped to

meet us. I said my prayers and braced for impact. I wasn't cold any longer. I didn't feel anything at all except adrenaline rushing through my body. After what felt like too long, I opened my eyes. I saw the nose of the raft inch ever so slightly to the right, toward deeper water.

"Go! Go! Go!" the guys chanted as Slingshot and I doubled our pace.

The raft slipped around, its back end missing the rocks by inches as we pivoted safely into a bottomless pool formed by the ancient walls. Inside the gorge, the whistling died away.

"Close shave," said Dad as Slingshot and I hunched over our paddles, gasping for breath. "Nice work, boys!"

"Boys, boys, boys," came the echo.

I looked up, and all I could see was granite. The other rafts had disappeared. Around the bend, I hoped . . . and not to the bottom. Damp, mossy walls so tight I could almost touch either side of the river with my paddle rose straight up to a distant ribbon of sky. It felt like we had been washed to the bottom of a very deep well. The water was calmer in the belly of the chasm. It gave us a chance to catch our breath.

"Whistling Gorge," panted Slingshot. "That's what the wailing was. Wind funneling through the narrow canyon."

Stump blushed brighter than the red hair under his baseball cap.

"I thought the guys up ahead were playing tricks," he said. "Sorry!"

"Sorry, sorry, sorry," repeated the gorge.

"Once is enough," I said with a grin. "We get it already."

"Are you talking to Stump or the echo?" Slingshot asked.

"Stump," I said. "But the gorge has a lot to apologize for, too. It almost sank us!"

We pushed ahead, letting the current guide us safely down the main river channel until we popped free of the gorge like a butterfly emerging from its cocoon. It felt good to get back into the sunlight. Even better was the sight of two rafts dipping and weaving like corks a couple hundred yards in front of us. Everyone had made it through Whistling Gorge.

Free of the cliffs, the river spread out once again, wide and glittery, as it flowed through thick pine forest. A half hour of easy paddling nearly caught us up to everybody else—close enough, anyway, to see they were dogging it, legs trailing in the water, hats pulled over their eyes for shade as they reclined against the sides of their rafts.

Mr. Bones barked a greeting. Heads popped up like Whack-A-Moles as the guys stirred themselves just long enough to peek over the gunwales at us. We followed in their lazy wake until we came to a sandy crescent on a curve in the river, a natural spot to go ashore. We pulled our raft up on the beach behind the others and discovered a weathered picnic table and a stone fire circle tucked back from the water amid a grove of hemlocks.

"The campsite at Tinkham Woods," Dad

announced. "We made it."

We cheered.

"Who's up for a swim?" asked Mr. James, stripping off his T-shirt.

We whooped again as we raced down the beach and splashed into the cool, clear water. After paddling on top of the river for so long, it felt amazing to jump right down into it.

Between swimming and setting up camp, the rest of the afternoon passed quickly. Stump, Slingshot, and I pitched our gray-and-purple nylon tent in a flat, grassy spot at the edge of the woods. The other guys fanned outward around us, forming a semicircle of domed tents whose flaps opened toward the fire pit. With the tents up, our encampment looked like a small village of high-tech igloos.

We laid out our sleeping bags, then scavenged for firewood. Meanwhile, our dads organized our cooking area. They set up the portable stove near the picnic table and stowed our chest-sized blue-and-white coolers of drinks and meat within easy reach. The rest of the food—granola, fruit, crackers, marsh-mallows, hamburger and hot dog buns—they packed into mesh bags and hung from tree branches several healthy paces away from the tents.

"Why can't we just leave it on the table, where we can get at it?" Gilly complained.

"Because if we did, I guarantee you it would be gone by morning," answered his dad.

"We won't eat *everything*," promised Gilly.

"You might not. But bears will."

"Bears?" Gilly gulped.

"The park's thick with them. If food's easy to grab, they'll take it. On the table, say, or in a tent. If it's out of reach, they'll mosey along."

Without another word, Gilly whipped a Her-shey bar out of his pocket and tossed it into one of the bags. He then scoured the site for anything remotely edible and tucked it away. "Bears," he muttered. "Bad news, bears." By the time he finished, there was not so much as one loose peanut to be found within a mile.

With the camp shipshape, we started a crackling fire and began grilling hamburgers and roasting hot dogs. I did not forget my promise to Mr. Bones. He likes his burgers medium rare. Actually, he likes them any old way at all, including, as we found out when Dad started showing off with the spatula, flipped onto the ground by mistake and rolled in pine needles.

I chuckled and scratched him behind the ears.

As the sun sank into the forest, we tucked into dinner. Between mouthfuls, we talked about the championship game against the Hog City Haymakers that awaited us back in Rambletown.

"Flicker Pringle has been lights out since the All-Star Game," said the Glove. "I don't think he's given up so much as a bloop single in ten games."

Flicker Pringle is Hog City's pitcher. The guy is beyond good. He hurls the ball so fast you can't even see it. You hear a *whoosh* like a steam train, then a firecracker pop as it explodes into the catcher's mitt. That is, unless it slams into you. Flicker believes he owns the plate. If he thinks a batter is crowding it, he's more than willing to play a little chin music.

"Aww, Flicker Pringle doesn't scare me," said Ocho. "We'll beat him like a drum. We've done it once already this year."

It was true. We had. Way back on opening day, when snow still lay deep on the ground, we'd come from behind to clip the Haymakers. Of course, a few weeks after that they'd trounced us 11–3 in our worst loss of the season. We hadn't played them since.

"I'll take us over the Haymakers any day," continued Ocho, "so long as the weather holds."

At the mention of weather, I glanced across the flickering fire at Slingshot. He sat on a rock and gazed into the flames. I could tell he was brooding about his weird pitching slump, how every time he touched the ball the only thing that rose faster than his ERA was floodwater from the pelting rain. On the other hand, it had been dry all day. Even now the stars shone brightly in the velvety night sky. Then again, Slingshot hadn't thrown a baseball for a while.

"There's the Big Dipper," I said, changing the subject. "And the little one, too."

Everybody craned their necks and scanned the night sky.

"Ursa Major and Ursa Minor," said Slingshot.

"More bears!" Gilly shuddered. "We can't seem to get away from those critters."

"Bears I can handle," said Tugboat. "It's the Devil's Furnace I'm worried about. If it's anything like Whistling Gorge, we're in for a wild ride tomorrow."

"When do we start looking for the treasure?" said Billy, leaning forward eagerly on the log where he sat. "Can you imagine the look on Joe Wood's face when we show up with the gold?"

"What cave? What gold?" asked Mr. Wishes. "Who in the world is Joe Wood?"

We told about meeting the guide. How he had searched for the Moonlight Bandit's lost hoard when he was a kid.

"You believe that old ghost story?" asked Mr. Wishes.

"Maybe not all of it," Billy admitted. "But the bandit was real. The only mystery is what became of him. He couldn't have just disappeared into thin air."

"Of course not," said Ocho. "The stranger in black got him. Everybody knows that."

He whipped out a flashlight and clicked it under his chin, lighting up his face demonically from below. "Canoe and all, the Moonlight Bandit plunged down, down, down into the reeking bowels of the earth," he recited, making his voice all spooky. "He came out in some kind of a weird underground forge, where a strange man he'd never seen before greeted him as if he'd been expected."

Mr. Bones buried his head in my lap. He's a dog who likes to be petted and likes to lick faces. He does not like creepy strangers lurking in freaky caves or highwaymen who barter their souls. Not even ones who vanished hundreds of years ago.

"Flames licked the hot stones," continued Ocho. "The fire glowed brighter and brighter. The stranger's eyes glittered as the bandit pleaded for mercy. And to this day, his fearful cries still ring!"

"Whew." Velcro shuddered. "That story gives me the chills every time I hear it."

"You want to hear a really scary story?" I asked. As long as we were in campfire mode, I had a good one.

Everybody nodded.

"It happened not long ago, in a town not far from here," I began. "One day a boy, a baseball player, it so happens, just the same age as we are, was forced to clean out the attic by his cruel father."

"Wait a minute!" My dad laughed. "Is this a true story?"

"Just listen. The attic was hotter than an oven. Dusty piles of junk filled every corner. Cobwebs hung from the rafters. What the boy wouldn't have given for a drink of cool water!

"As he sifted through the mounds of long-forgotten junk, he came upon a bent and battered umbrella. The fabric was black. The shaft and spokes were made of bamboo. Although he recognized many things in the attic, the boy could not remember ever having seen the umbrella. Curious, he carelessly opened it. As he did, his hands tingled as if he'd caught an electric eel by the tail. At that very moment he remembered the ancient curse: He who unfurls an umbrella inside a house shall unleash a torrent of bad luck.

"Quickly the boy threw the umbrella to the floor. He went back to work and tried to forget about it. With all his might, he tried to forget what he had done. But he could not.

"Later that very day, after finishing his job in the attic, he went off to play baseball. But no sooner than the game started did rain come crashing down. And every day thereafter, whenever the boy played baseball, the rain came.

I paused for dramatic effect, then shouted:

"And it was all because of *this*!"

I whipped out the old umbrella, which I had hidden behind the log I was sitting on.

"*Aaieeeee!*" screamed the guys, playing along. "The haunted umbrella! The haunted umbrella. It must be destroyed!"

"Did that really happen?" asked Billy.

"Well, I did find the umbrella in the attic over our garage, and I did make the mistake of opening it. And, well, you know about all the rain."

"Cruel father, huh?" said my dad with a chuckle. "Well, I think that's a little harsh. But I will agree there's only one way out of this. We've got to burn that thing to cinders!"

"Can we?" I asked.

"Can't hurt," he said.

We let Slingshot do the honors. To the cheer of the guys, he snapped the umbrella into pieces and fed it bit by bit into the campfire. As he did, he looked over at me and smiled knowingly.

When nothing remained but ash, we all turned in for the night. I don't know if the umbrella was truly cursed or not. But baseball is a superstitious game, and there's not a player in the world who would go out of his way to tempt fate. Plus, like Dad said, getting rid of the thing couldn't do any harm. All I know is, I was happy when it was gone.

I zipped the tent flap behind me, said good night to Stump and Slingshot, and crawled into my sleeping bag.

"Thanks, Walloper," said Slingshot from across the darkness.

I remembered the time he had cooked up a crazy séance to cure me of a batting slump.

"That umbrella has been bugging me," I said.

The last thing I heard before drifting off was Gilly in the tent next to ours.

"How about toothpaste?" he called. "Do bears eat toothpaste? Should I get rid of this tube?"

I pulled my bag up around my ears and went to sleep.

# ★ CHAPTER 14 ★

I awoke to the smell of wood smoke and frying bacon.

Rubbing sleep from my eyes, I sat up and fumbled with the tent flaps. Stump, Slingshot, and I crawled out of our zippered dome, one behind the other. Mr. Bones didn't bother to wait in line. He leapfrogged over us and dashed to the fire, where Dad was hunched over the cookstove, wreathed in smoke. Mist rose from the river. Sunlight filtered through pine branches. There wasn't a cloud in the sky.

"Good morning, slugabeds!" bellowed Mr. Plumwhiff from the picnic table, where he and the other grown-ups sat sipping coffee. "Glad you could join us!"

"What time is it?" mumbled Stump.

"Getting late," said his dad. "Almost six in the a.m.!"

"Your timing is uncanny," said my dad. "Breakfast will be ready in five minutes. Bacon, omelets, and camp toast with maple syrup. You have time for a quick dip if you want one. Nothing like it for getting the blood pumping!"

Sounded like a good idea to me. I darted back into the tent and slipped into my swim trunks. Stump and Slingshot followed. We raced down to the river and plunged in up to our necks. Our shouts soon woke up the rest of the team.

"How's the water?" asked Gasser, stumbling down the path with a beach towel draped around his neck.

"Perfect," I said through chattering teeth. "You just have to jump in without thinking about it."

He did. Everybody did. A water rumble quickly broke out. It was like free swim at the community pool, only a million times better. The lifeguards don't allow chicken fights at the pool.

"Grub's on!" hollered Mr. James. "Come and get it!"

Fully awake, we splashed up the beach and trundled across the soft, pine-matted earth to breakfast.

"Lumberjack special," said my dad, sliding a whopper of an omelet off the griddle. The thing was huge. If one of our rafts sank, we could ride the omelet down the river to the ranger station.

Dad carved up his creation and served it on paper plates. Molten cheese oozed from the sides like lava. He handed off the plates to Mr. Plumwhiff, who topped each one with a couple of bacon slices and a hunk of fried bread. "Syrup's on the table," he said. "And bug juice."

Breakfast never tasted so good. Bacon, eggs, and toast on the banks of a mountain river beat Pirate Crunch cereal at home any day of the week.

After we ate, Dad spread out a map on the picnic table.

"We're here," he said. "The ranger station is here. In between lies the Devil's Furnace."

We stretched our necks to look.

"How long to get there? Couple hours, do you figure?" asked Mr. Winkle, Kid Rabbit's dad.

"Sounds about right," Dad answered. "Before we make our run through the rapids, I'm thinking we might want to reconnoiter at this island." He thumbed a sliver of land in the middle of the river.

"Good idea," agreed Mr. Winkle. "We can collect ourselves, make sure the rafts are in order. Maybe take one last dip before we hit the whitewater."

We all nodded. A swim before the Devil's Furnace sounded good. A swim in the Devil's

Furnace? Not so much. I hoped we'd be up to the challenge of the infamous rapids.

"Well then, let's get cracking!"

We broke camp and loaded up the rafts. It was not yet eight in the morning when we shoved off, Mr. Bones once again standing in the bow like George Washington crossing the Delaware. On a normal summer day I'd probably still be in bed. I was glad I wasn't. I would have missed the bald eagle that soared overhead minutes after we hit the river. With its fierce eyes and hooked beak, there was no mistaking it. It looked exactly like all the pictures you've ever seen.

"Amazing!" I said.

"Wing span of seven feet," said Slingshot.

Keeping our eyes peeled for wildlife, we coasted over the riffling water. Slingshot kept up a running commentary: belted kingfisher, great blue heron, common merganser.

I may not be great at identifying birds, but I had no trouble at all recognizing the animal that stood in a stretch of marshy shallows as we rounded a bend.

"Moose!" I exclaimed.

The thing was the size of a cabin. Its legs were so long you could've driven an ice-cream truck under its body. From the tip of one fuzzy antler to the other was a long-distance phone call. Mr. Bones was so awed he forgot to bark.

The moose raised its head, water streaming from its muzzle, and stared back at us with enormous dark eyes. It didn't seem to think much of what it saw. Certainly we didn't alarm it. He knew he was the king and we were mere flotsam drifting through his domain. With a snort, he returned to his meal of water plants.

"Whoa," whispered Stump. "It's bigger even than Hoot Fewster."

I snorted.

Hoot plays first base for the Hog City Haymakers. He's a living, breathing mountain of humanity. Biggest kid I've ever seen in my life. Stand him next to the moose, and he would have looked like something that belonged on a charm bracelet.

The river carried us downstream, and before long a low island appeared in the water. We paddled over to it and saw that it was more of a gravel bar than a true island, low and flat with a tangle of brush sprouting near its crown. We beached our rafts and dragged them up onto the gravel. I couldn't believe two hours had already passed.

"You sure this is the place?" I asked.

"Has to be," Dad said. "There's only one island between the campsite and the Devil's Furnace."

I exchanged a glance with Stump. I could tell the name gave him tingles, same as it did me. The place was so close now we could feel it.

We downed some bug juice and had a snack. A few of the guys broke out fishing rods and hiked down the beach to try their luck casting. I stayed at the island with the others, to horse around in the shallows.

On the gravel beach, Billy picked up a flat stone and sent it skipping across the surface. One, two, three, four splashes.

"Not bad!" I shouted.

He tossed another. Then Gasser whipped a beauty that splashed seven times before drowning. It didn't take long before our competitive instincts took over and a contest broke out. I snagged a stone with my toes and brought it to the surface. Standing waist deep, I hurled it sidearm across the current. It skipped once and flew a good twenty feet before landing with a tiny splash.

"Quality," I gloated. "Not quantity."

"Oh, yeah? Watch this," called Tugboat, who proceeded to jump one nearly all the way to the far bank. "First guy to get one across wins!" he challenged.

Slingshot grabbed a handful of skimmers and whipped them rapid-fire, Wyatt Earp at the O.K. Corral. As he did, a threatening cloud passed in front of the sun.

*Uh-oh*, I thought.

Slingshot tossed another stone.

"Stop!" I shouted. "It's happening again!"

Too late.

The sky opened and rain pelted down, pocking the water like shotgun blasts. In an instant, the color of the river changed from silvery blue to battleship gray. Then it rose in a frightening cola-brown froth that swept clear over our low island. We sloshed to the rafts before the angry current carried them away. In the mad rush, we didn't bother getting organized. There wasn't time. It was every man for himself, and we all just jumped into whichever boat was closest.

I found myself hurtling down the swollen river with Stump, Slingshot, Billy, Gilly, and Velcro. Mr. Bones huddled against my legs. The rain crashed upon us like a wall, sealing us off from the other boats. I couldn't see more than ten feet in front of my face. I felt like I was trapped inside a giant bottle of soda that some prankster was furiously shaking.

A real bottle would have been nice. We could have cut it in half and used it to bail the raft, which was quickly taking on water.

"Caps," I shouted. "Use your ball caps to scoop up water!"

Someone was moaning.

"Don't worry, Billy," I said. "We won't sink." I thought the kid was sobbing. I didn't blame him. I felt plenty scared myself.

"I know we won't!" he called, his voice ringing clear.

Who was crying?

The sound got louder and louder, a spine-tingling wail. Even in the lashing rain, my hair stood on end.

The words of Joe Wood came back to me.

"Listen to the river," he'd said.

At the moment it sounded like nothing on earth. It sounded haunted.

That was it!

Haunted!

The Devil's Furnace! At long last, we had

entered the infamous rapids. Nothing else could explain the spooky moan of wind and water or the way the river boiled and seethed.

Not only that, but we had arrived in a torrential downpour, just as the Moonlight Bandit before us.

Our raft buckled and bumped over sunken boulders. We paddled furiously, but we might as well have been using toothpicks. The rapids had us in their grip and would not let go.

Suddenly a towering pile of rocks loomed out of the water, smack in front of us. As the current flung us toward it, the hideous shrieking reached a deafening pitch. The raft began to twirl. I felt like a blob of paint on a spin-art wheel.

A very small, very frightened blob of pale white paint in a swirling sea of brown and gray.

The rocks flashed closer and closer.

"Hold on, guys!" I shouted. "We're going to . . ."

As I spoke, we lurched wildly. I reached for

something to grab, anything that would keep me in the boat.

Then everything went dark, and we began to fall.

# ★ CHAPTER 15 ★

**T**he raft crashed with a bone-rattling jolt, and I bounced off its rubber bottom and rose through the air. A second later, I landed on something soft and lumpy.

"Whoever just jumped on me, please get off," came Stump's muffled voice.

"Sorry," I said. I heaved myself forward. It was pitch-black. I couldn't see a thing. "Is everybody okay? Where the heck are we?"

"We're on land," said Velcro. "I feel sand."

"I think it stopped raining," said Gilly.

"I never should have thrown those rocks," said Slingshot. "I'm sorry, guys. I wanted to see what would happen. I guess now we know."

"We know nothing," insisted Stump.

"I don't even know where we are," said Velcro.

"Mr. Bones!" I called.

Something wet touched my face in the dark. Two paws pressed against my chest. Mr. Bones barked.

"Good boy!" I said.

The moaning had stopped. Water pounded somewhere nearby. The air was warm and dry.

"We need to find the waterproof bag," I said. "The camp lantern and our phones are in it."

Gingerly, on hands and knees, we felt around for our gear.

"Careful," I said. For all I knew, we could have been crawling blindly at the edge of a cliff.

"Found something!" cried Gilly.

"My foot," said Billy

"No, I really did!" insisted Gilly.

"I know," said his little brother. "You found my foot."

We laughed. A moment later, Slingshot brushed against the actual bag. He unzippered it and fumbled for the battery-powered lantern.

"Let's hope this thing still works," he said. "Here goes nothing."

He hit the switch. The lantern glowed to life, revealing the inside of a cave. A quick look around showed us the place was shaped like a football, narrow at both ends and fat in the middle.

Our raft lay overturned at one end, its back end floating in a narrow stream that ran along the near wall of the cave. Bags and coolers lay strewn all over the sandy floor. Yellow quartz glittered in the walls, which climbed straight up on all sides. Stalactites glistened like icicles from the ceiling.

"Whoa!" said Stump, speaking for all of us.

"How did we get in here?" Billy wondered.

Slingshot clambered to his feet and raised the lantern, casting light high up the walls.

"There," he said, pointing. Not far from where we'd come to rest, a thick column of water sloshed down from the darkness above. It cascaded off slick ledges as it plunged, collecting in a pool at the bottom before draining into the stream.

"There has to be a crevice in the rocks we ran into on the river," Slingshot guessed. "Water flows through it when the river's flooding. We were launched into it and must have tumbled over the waterfall and landed here."

"In the Devil's Furnace," said Stump with a whistle. "Just like the story says."

We all nervously huddled together a little bit closer, as if the ring of lamplight could protect us from whatever lurked in the darkness.

"When the river is running at a normal level, the entrance must be too high to reach from the outside," Slingshot said. "But in a heavy downpour, the water rises really quickly and washes over an opening in the rocks."

"Nobody in their right mind would tackle

the Big Fork when it's flooding," said Gilly. "So no one ever discovered the crevice."

"Nobody but the Moonlight Bandit," said Velcro.

"And us," added Stump. "I guess we're crazy enough."

"Out of the frying pan and into the fire," Gilly said nervously.

"At least it's not broiling hot," said Billy. "Like in the story."

"So how do we get out?" asked Gilly, eyeing the ceiling. "There's no way to reach the opening from down here without a ladder. A really long ladder."

I craned my neck. I could not see the top of the waterfall. "Hand me my phone," I said.

"Why?" asked Stump. "You have a ladder app on it or something?"

"We've got to let the others know where we are," I said.

Slingshot passed me my phone from the bag and I speed-dialed my dad. Nothing happened.

I checked the screen. No bars.

"I can't get a signal," I announced. "Someone else try."

While the guys with phones gave it a shot, I inched over to the base of the waterfall to see if there might be some way to scale the walls.

"Nothing," announced Stump. "The phones are useless down here."

Tentatively, I wedged my toe into a small crack in the rocks and tried to hoist myself up. I made it about six inches before crashing back down.

"No chance," I said. "It's too slippery. We'll never get out this way."

"Like I said," Gilly shuddered. "We need a ladder."

Slingshot swung the lantern in an arc, lighting up more of the cave. Suddenly he froze. On the far wall, stalagmites and stalactites joined together in a weird formation. From where we stood, it looked exactly like a giant fireplace.

"Yipes!" cried Billy. "It's real!"

Mr. Bones charged across the cave, barking wildly.

"Come back, boy!" I yelled as he disappeared into the shadows.

He didn't listen. Without thinking, I darted after him. Before I knew it, I found myself standing next to the fireplace. Its mouth gaped wide and tall, more than large enough for a man to duck inside. Mr. Bones danced at the opening. I grabbed his collar before he could lunge into the recess in the rocks.

"Bring the light," I called to the guys. "Hurry!"

My teammates raced over, the lantern casting eerie shadows as they ran.

"What is it, Mr. Bones?" I asked, my voice trembling with excitement. "What did you find?"

"A way out, I hope," said Velcro.

Slingshot thrust the lantern into the hollow place. Suddenly, the light washed over a hairy black mass. The thing was large and lumpy. It looked ready to pounce. My heart played hopscotch in my chest.

"Bear!" shrieked Gilly. "Run!"

He didn't have to say it twice. I was already backpedaling as fast as I could. So were the others. We fell all over ourselves trying to get out of the way.

"Wait," called Slingshot. "It's not a bear! It's bearskins!"

"You sure?" asked Gilly suspiciously. "It could be a bear playing possum."

"That makes no sense at all," said Stump.

"You know what makes no sense?" Gilly asked. "Surviving a plunge into the Devil's Furnace only to get eaten by a sneaky bear, that's what!"

"It's just skins," Slingshot assured us. "Honest. Come see. It looks like there's something else in there, too!"

Cautiously we crept back to the alcove. Slingshot was right. It was a bundle of furs, all right. A massive one, easily the size of all six of our sleeping bags laid one atop the other.

"Look!" Slingshot pointed the lantern. "Next to the pelts."

I craned my neck. There, half buried in the sand, lay the battered wooden ribs of a ruined canoe.

"Holy moly," whistled Stump. "It's true. The legend really is true!"

We grabbed the cracked leather thongs that bound the bundle of furs together and dragged it out of the hiding place.

"Heavy!" grunted Stump. "The bandit was nuts to try to run the rapids with such a humongous load."

"Assuming these ever were the bandit's," said Slingshot.

"Who else could have brought them here?" Velcro asked.

"Let's open them," suggested Billy. "The gold must be rolled up inside somewhere."

As I may have mentioned earlier, Billy is the

luckiest kid I know. He's always finding stuff. If he wanted to look for long-lost treasure inside a musty old pile of black bear furs, who was I to stop him?

With trembling hands, we loosened the knots and began shaking out the thick furs one at a time. They were matted and dusty after sitting in the cave for a couple hundred years, but otherwise in surprisingly good shape. I could imagine one spread on the floor in front of a crackling fire in a mountain lodge.

The pile got smaller. When we reached the last pelt, Stump flapped it like a towel. No golden coins cascaded to the floor.

"Nothing." Stump sighed. "Where could they be?"

"Maybe there is no gold," I said.

"There has to be," insisted Stump. "Everything else in the story is accurate. It's here somewhere. I know it."

Suddenly I had an idea.

"Slingshot," I said. "You don't still happen to

have that willow branch Joe Wood gave you, do you?"

"The dowsing rod?" he said. "Sure. It's in my pack. I saved it as a souvenir. Why?"

"Of course!" said Gilly. "Joe said dowsers use them to find metal!"

"That's pure superstition," Slingshot said. "You don't really believe in it, do you?"

"Probably it is mumbo jumbo," I agreed. "But seeing as we're kind of stuck here, what's the harm in trying?"

"You guys are nuts." Slingshot sighed as he trudged across the cave to the boat to find his pack.

"Don't keep us in the dark," called Gilly. "Hurry back with the lantern!"

Slingshot returned in a minute, holding the dowsing rod at arm's length like a pair of smelly underpants.

"Here," he said, thrusting the forked branch into Billy's hands. "You've always been lucky. You give it a whirl."

Billy took the stick and began walking slowly back and forth near the fireplace. Holding our breath, we watched intently. He reached the recess where we'd found the canoe and turned around.

"Nothing," he said with a shake of his head.

"Really," said Slingshot. "That is such a surprise."

Suddenly Billy jerked to a stop.

"I felt something!" he cried. "It twitched! Right here!"

We fell on the ground at his feet and began pawing at the dirt. "Mr. Bones," I called. "You're a dog. Get over here and dig!"

He bounded between us and went at it like a steam shovel. Dirt flew between his legs and piled up behind him. In two minutes, the hole was a foot deep. A second after that, his nails clinked against something metallic.

"Whoa, boy!" I cried, wrapping my arms around his neck. "That's enough!"

He licked my face excitedly.

"Shine the light in there," cried Gilly.

Slingshot lowered the lantern.

I gasped.

At the bottom of the hole, a pile of gleaming gold coins spilled out of a split leather bag.

"We found it!" hollered Stump, scooping up a handful. "We really found it!"

We picked up the coins, carefully sifting through the dirt to make sure we got each one. There were forty-six in all. Each one was round and heavy and stamped with the image of a fat-faced guy wearing a leafy branch in his long, flowing curls. A royal-looking shield full of prancing lions graced the backside. Foreign writing, Latin, I guessed, spelled out the name GEORGIUS II.

"George the Second," said Slingshot. "An English king!"

"By George, we're rich!" exclaimed Stump.

"Like that'll do us a lot of good down here," I said, suddenly remembering where we were. "Apparently it didn't do much good for the Moonlight Bandit."

Our celebration came to a screeching halt.

"You're right," said Gilly. "We've got to find a way out."

"Speaking of the bandit," said Velcro, "we found everything else. But where did he go?"

We all turned to the fireplace.

# ★ CHAPTER 16 ★

"**D**o you really think . . ."

We huddled at the base of the weird rocks that looked like a fireplace.

"Only one way to find out," said Slingshot.

He bravely stuck his head inside the opening.

"Guys, I can see light way up at the top! This thing really is like a chimney."

Slingshot set down the lantern and pulled himself up into the rocks until his feet dangled above the ground.

"Narrow," came his muffled voice. "Wait a minute, what's this?"

He dropped back to the ground and emerged

from the fireplace holding a metal wedge. We crowded around for a closer look.

"The head of a hatchet!" said Gilly. "I think we can say for sure which way the trapper went."

"Hold on to it," said Slingshot. "I'm going back up."

He ducked inside the chimney again and began climbing. Lying on our backs with our heads inside the fireplace, we watched as he inched his way up the narrow passage. His swinging feet dislodged pebbles, sending a shower of grit our way.

"Careful!" said Stump.

"Trying," answered Slingshot. "It's getting really tight. I don't know how much farther I can make it."

My heart sank like an anchor. How else could we escape?

Suddenly Slingshot yelped.

"What?" I hollered.

"I'm coming down! I'm coming down!"

We barely had time to clear out of the way before he dropped heavily onto the floor of the chimney, loose debris rattling down with him.

"What is it? What happened?"

Slingshot was panting. Dirt streaked his face. His elbows and knees were scraped.

"I found something else," he said.

"Tell me it's more gold," said Billy.

Slingshot grabbed the lantern and shined it into the fireplace. A long white stick with knobs on both ends rested on the sand where it had fallen.

"Some kind of war club?" asked Gilly doubtfully.

In the same instant Slingshot shook his head, I recognized the thing in the fireplace and shuddered. It was a bone.

"There are more up there," Slingshot whispered. "Wedged into the rocks. I touched them."

"Yowza! I guess we know what became of the bandit," said Velcro.

"He tried to climb out and got stuck," I said.

"Oh, man, that's horrible!" Gilly shivered.

"Let's get out of here!" shouted Billy.

We all nodded. The question was—how?

There was no way up the waterfall, and the chimney was too narrow. That left the far end of the cave. We would have to go that way and hope for a break.

We picked up our scattered gear and packed what we might need into the dry bag, along with our dads' car keys, wallets, and phones. And the coins, of course. We wouldn't be leaving those behind.

Our useful supplies didn't amount to much. A couple of water bottles, some two-day-old PB&Js sealed in plastic bags, half a chocolate bar, and a jackknife. Billy asked if he could keep his lucky baseball cards. I didn't see why not. They were light. And we needed all the luck we could muster. Slingshot held on to the ax head. The bone we left in the fireplace.

Everything else—sleeping bags, paddles— we piled in the raft, which we pulled all the way out of the shallow stream that trickled along one edge of the cave. If we ever made it out, we could always come back later for that stuff.

Keeping to the edge of the stream, we started walking.

"We're in good shape," I said. "This brook has to lead somewhere. It can't stay underground forever."

I sure hoped I was right.

We quickly passed out of the large chamber. The cave grew narrower and lower. It twisted to the left and right. To keep our spirits up, we tried singing. "Ninety-Nine Bottles of Root Beer on the Wall" somehow didn't fit the mood, though a real root beer would've been nice. We were low on drinking water. The pirate song "Yo Ho Ho and a Bottle of Rum" seemed more appropriate. It's full of scoundrels and skeletons and plunder.

After a while, the passage became so narrow we had to walk single file. Carrying the lantern, Slingshot squeezed in front. Ever since we'd fallen into the cave, I'd noticed, he'd been leading the way. Maybe he thought it was his responsibility to get us out safely because he blamed himself for our predicament. Slingshot was a natural leader. All I know is I would have followed him anywhere. Including into battle against the Hog City Haymakers. But that would have to wait. At the moment we still had to find a way out of the cave.

Soon the passage narrowed further and we had no choice but to slosh through the stream. The water was shin deep and cold. Really cold. Mr. Bones splashed through it like a sheepdog keeping his flock in order. The rest of us scuttled like crabs, bent double under the low sloping ceiling. A real crab would have been nice. It would have fit my mood perfectly.

Velcro stopped without warning, and I bumped him from behind.

"Listen," he said.

At first I heard nothing, but gradually I

picked up a faint hum.

"Running water," he said. "I think we're near the river."

We cheered like mad and pushed ahead, through narrower and narrower gaps. Soon the walls and floor changed from solid rock to soft, dark mud that came away in handfuls when you steadied yourself against it. The stream seeped away into the earth. Tree roots appeared in the ceiling, interlaced with stones and soil. The passage was no larger than a sewer pipe, and only slightly less appealing to burrow through.

"Boulder," Slingshot said, stopping again. "Help me loosen it."

He passed the lantern down the line and I squeezed next to him, my head jamming into wet dirt. I helped Slingshot scrape around the edges of a giant rock that protruded from the ceiling, blocking our way. The earth gave way, and the boulder collapsed with a wet sucking sound. Light poured through the void it left behind.

"We're out!" I shouted, gulping fresh air.

Slingshot first, the rest of us popped up through the hole and into a mossy, boulder-strewn forest. If anyone had been there to see us, they would have thought we were a family of very strange moles. I know I felt like one. A very dirty, very tired, and very happy mole.

The minute we came out of the ground, our bag of supplies started beeping like a mutant alarm clock.

"The phones!" I said.

I tore open the bag and grabbed the first one I could find. It started ringing as soon as I touched it.

"Hello!" I answered.

"Banjie!"

It was my dad.

"Are you all right?" he cried. "Where are you?"

"Right here," I said.

I started sprinting through the trees. The guys and Mr. Bones raced with me, all of us whooping like mad. The cave had led us to within a hundred yards of the ranger station, where I could see my dad, all of our dads, huddled in the parking lot around a park truck, its roof lights flashing. The ranger from the day we drove into the park was there, still wearing his Smokey the Bear hat. Joe Wood was there, looking serious, along with a whole lot of other people I didn't know. A search party, I guessed.

We burst out of the woods and into the biggest group hug the North Woods has ever seen. My dad squeezed me so hard I thought I would burst. Nothing ever felt better.

After we calmed down, we told everybody about the cave and what we had found in it. We opened the bag and showed them the coins, just so they would know we weren't making it up.

Joe Wood's eyes lit up like the Fourth of July.

"I knew it!" he exclaimed. Mr. Bones leaped up and licked his face.

We marched everyone through the woods to our tunnel. A park official snapped pictures of us standing in front of the entrance, caked in mud and smiling like we'd just won the World Series.

"I'm guessing none of you probably is too keen on leading me down this hole?" Joe asked.

We shook our heads.

"It's time for us to get home," said my dad. "Our families are waiting."

"Just keep going straight," I told Joe. "You'll come to the main chamber. You can't miss it. A person could live down there, it's so big. You'll find the canoe and everything, just like we told you."

"A crazy person could live there, you mean," said Stump. "Personally, I plan to stay above-ground from now on."

The guide nodded. "I don't blame you," he said.

"What about all the stuff we left down there?" Velcro asked. "Our sleeping bags, the raft?"

"Don't worry about any of that," said Joe.

"Now that we know how to get in, we'll want to plan a careful excavation. We'll get your stuff out eventually. Along with everything else." His eyes twinkled. "I can't tell you how excited I am to see the artifacts. We'll put the canoe and the furs, if we can salvage them, in a museum. The coins, well, I don't know what the rules are about who gets to keep treasure found on public land. At the very least, I think you should be entitled to a nice reward."

We shook hands all around and said our good-byes. The guys started back for the parking lot, but I lingered for a moment longer.

"Actually," I said, "I think there is something you could do for us."

"Name it," said Joe.

"You know that thing about dowsing you told us? The forked willow sticks and all?"

I looked over my shoulder to make sure no one was listening. Then I leaned close and whispered my idea.

A sly smile spread across Joe's face.

"It just might work," he said.

I borrowed a pen from him and scribbled Gabby's name and phone number on the back of a trail map.

"She'll know what to do," I said. "There's a good one near the bike rack just outside the field."

Then I turned and ran after the others.

I was eager to get back to Rambletown. We had a championship baseball game to play.

# ★ CHAPTER 17 ★

The next morning, the Rounders moved out of the sports section and onto the front page of the *Rambletown Bulletin*.

A big color picture showed Slingshot holding up a gold coin as the rest of us looked on. The banner headline over it proclaimed:

*Local Kids Uncover*
*Lost Treasure of the North Woods*
*Mystery of "Moonlight Bandit" Solved!*

The article took up the whole page and continued inside the paper. I was deep into it when my dad interrupted with a cry of "Breakfast!"

He lumbered over to the kitchen table bearing a giant omelet on a platter. Mr. Bones danced at his feet. Dad had cut his creation into a circle and sprinkled two curved lines of red paprika across the top of it to make the thing look like a baseball. A moon-sized baseball.

"You've outdone yourself," said Mom.

"In honor of today's game," he said. "There's hits in omelets, you know."

He always said that. Maybe he even believed it. I hoped the Haymakers were tucking into pancakes. Something without hits in it.

Dad set down the platter. The table swayed but held fast.

He returned to the kitchen counter and switched on the radio. Instantly the voice of Louie "the Lip" Leibenstraub filled the room.

"It's a beautiful day for baseball," the DJ said. "Clear skies as far as the eye can see. Speaking of baseball, in case you've been living under a rock or something, there's a big showdown today between Rambletown's own Rounders, fresh from their wilderness conquest, and the Hog City Haymakers. This next number goes out to our hometown heroes! Good luck, guys! Keep on slugging . . . and keep your dials tuned to WHOT 102.5!"

The rocking beat of "We Are the Champions" blasted from the speakers.

"I love this song!" Dad exclaimed. He started singing along to the radio. I laughed. It was good to be home.

"Did you sleep all right, Banjie?" Mom shouted over the ruckus. "I was worried about you."

"Like a rock," I said. Sometimes I get anxious before big games. But I was so exhausted when we got back from Abenaki that I forgot to toss and turn about the Haymakers. I'd fallen asleep the minute my head hit the pillow. Maybe I should start a new tradition of getting lost in caves before baseball games.

Maybe not.

After eating, I helped Mom put away the

breakfast things. Then I went up to my room and changed into my uniform. I couldn't believe it was the last time I'd ever wear the familiar red and white of the Rounders.

An hour before game time, I wheeled my bike out of the garage and hung my mitt on the handlebar. Mom and Dad wished me luck, promising to be in the bleachers good and late.

"Maybe extra late," said Dad. "Maybe as late as the third inning."

"Don't push it, honey," said Mom. "We'll see you in the second, Banjie."

With Mr. Bones trotting along at my wheel, I rode to meet Stump and Slingshot and Velcro. The pack of us cruised together to Rambletown Field. The field was dry when we got there, the base paths swept, and the grass freshly mowed. Red, white, and blue bunting draped the grandstand. The only sign of the recent deluge was a black high-water mark on the outfield wall. It stretched about two feet above the ground in an unbroken line from one end of the boards to the other. Maybe someday someone would put up a plaque to commemorate the historic Rambletown flood.

We ditched our bikes in the rack and hurried onto the field. At home plate we ran into Gabby Hedron, ponytail poking out the back of her Rounders cap, usual black notebook in hand.

"You guys are amazing," she said excitedly. "First you solve the mystery of the Devil's Furnace, now you're going to cook the Haymakers."

"We're going to try our best anyway," I said uneasily. It's never good to predict the outcome of a game.

"How do you feel, Slingshot?" she asked. "Ready to mow them down?" Gabby has her own way of looking at things.

Slingshot shrugged his shoulders. A worried look crossed his face like one of the rain clouds I hoped would not appear today.

"I tossed stones yesterday," he said grimly.

"You're sick?" Gabby gasped. "You threw up?"

"No, I literally tossed stones. I skipped them on the river."

"Oh, that's good," Gabby said with relief. "I thought you meant you had an upset stomach."

"It's not good," said Slingshot. "It started to rain. Hard. A total downpour."

"Coincidence," said Stump. "Nothing to it."

"I nearly got us killed," said Slingshot.

"He's crazy," I said. "He's the one who led us out of the cave. He saved our lives."

"I can already see the headline," said Gabby. "Hero Pitcher Rescues Teammates Twice!"

A smile flickered across Slingshot's lips. "We'll see," he said.

"We better go," I said. The rest of the team was already warming up.

The guys trotted out onto the field, but Gabby laid her hand on my arm and held me back.

"By the way," she whispered. "Early this morning I had a very interesting call from a park ranger named Joe Wood."

"Oh, good," I said. "Is he coming?"

"He's already here. He came with a truckload of supplies. We're taking care of everything."

"Thanks," I said. "I owe you one."

"Just play the game," she said. "We'll do the rest."

I turned and ran onto the field.

As we limbered up, the Haymakers gathered in front of their dugout and stared across the diamond at us. With their playoff beards and the trademark scowls that seemed as much a part of their uniforms as blue pinstripes, they made for an imposing sight. Hoot Fewster, their gargantuan first baseman, tried to intimidate us by flexing his muscles. He rippled like the Incredible Hulk's big brother. I had to reconsider my opinion. Maybe he wasn't so much smaller than that moose after all.

"Pray for rain," shouted Flicker Pringle. "It's the only way you'll avoid a butt kicking!"

His laughter rumbled like an earthquake.

We did our best to ignore those guys. It was

hard, though. They took up a lot of space.

"Let's bring it in, fellas," called Skip Lou, who must have sensed our faltering concentration.

We formed a ring around him, and he gave us the starting lineup.

"We're going to stick with the rotation that worked against Windsor," he announced. "Gilly will start, then we'll bring in Gasser for a couple innings."

We let this news sink in for a second. Slingshot had been benched. I looked over at my friend and watched his head drop.

Skip put his arm around the pitcher's shoulders.

"Don't worry," he said, trying to smooth things over. "You'll get your chance. You're our secret weapon. The Haymakers won't know what hit them when you come blazing off the bench."

Slingshot nodded without looking up. I knew exactly how he felt. I'd been scratched from a lineup before. It hurts. But you just have to suck it up and be ready to play when your number is called.

"Guys," continued Skip, "I want to say that it's been an honor and a pleasure to coach you all these years. However this game ends, you should know I'm proud of each and every one of you. Now go out there and have fun and give it your best. That's all I, or anyone, can ask. Do that, and you'll be winners no matter what."

He stuck his hand into the ring, and we piled ours on top.

"One, two, three—go Rounders!" we cried.

At home plate, the ump lowered his mask onto his face.

"PLAY BALL!" he barked.

A record crowd rose to its feet and cheered as we ran out onto the diamond.

# ★ CHAPTER 18 ★

Tugboat flashed the sign. Fastball. Gilly wound up and delivered the game's opening pitch. In the box, the colossal Haymaker leadoff man swung from his heels. The blast from his hack nearly blew me into the outfield from my position at third base. The guy was the size of a sequoia.

A real sequoia would have been nice. It would have knocked down the ball after it flew off the giant's bat. As it was, the ball sailed all the way into the center field bleachers.

One pitch, one swing, and just like that Hog City led by a run.

This was not the way we wanted to start the game.

"Shrug it off, Gilly," I called as Mr. Big Shot thundered around the bases. In the suddenly ghostly quiet ballpark, his footfalls reverberated like a pile driver.

Tugboat took a fresh ball from the ump and fired it to the mound. He flashed another sign. Changeup. I hoped it would work better than the fastball had.

The batter swung and missed.

"STEE-RIKE ONE!" bellowed the ump.

The batter whiffed on two more after that for the first out of the inning. Flicker Pringle followed him at the plate. From the dugout steps, Skip motioned for our outfielders to move back. Way back. All the way against the wall. Everybody knew that if there was one thing Flicker could do even better than throw the ball, it was hit the ball.

He took a practice swing, then pointed his enormous bat toward the flagpole beyond right field.

"That's where I'm going to dump this pitch," he snorted, in case anyone hadn't gotten his point.

He let Gilly's first pitch sail by for strike one, then held up a finger. When Gilly's next offering also crossed the plate, Flicker held up a second finger.

"One more now," I called. "One to strike him out!"

Gilly wound up and zipped a fastball. Flicker struck, all right. He just didn't strike out. He struck the ball so hard, it not only hit the flagpole, it nearly knocked it down.

"What did I tell you?" he said, flipping his bat and beginning a showboat jog around the bases.

Tugboat called time and loped out to the hill to talk to Gilly. I joined their confab.

"You okay?" Tugboat asked.

"Fine!" Gilly spit. He was as mad as I've ever seen him.

"Figured you were," said Tugboat.

"I almost feel sorry for the next guy," I said. "He's in for it."

Gilly didn't disappoint. He gathered himself and blazed three straight heaters into
Tugboat's mitt. When a new hitter stepped up,
he fired three more to end the top of the first
inning. The Haymakers had jumped out to an
early lead, but in the process they had angered
Gilly with their grandstanding.

You don't ever want to make Gilly mad. It
brings out the beast in him.

I hoped some of it would rub off on our bats.
If we were going to score against Flicker Pringle, we needed to be aggressive.

Ducks slapped on a helmet and strode up to
the plate.

On the mound, Flicker whipped his powerful right arm and launched a fastball. At least I
think he did. It moved so fast, I didn't actually
see anything. I heard plenty, though.

*WHOOSH!* went the pitch.

*"YOWCH!"* cried Hanky Burns, the Haymaker catcher, as the ball snapped into his
glove like a firecracker.

"STEE-RIKE ONE!" roared the ump.

The second pitch was like déjà vu. You had seen it before. Or not seen it, as was the usual case with a Flicker Pringle fastball. In any event, the result was the same.

"STRIKE TWO!" barked the ump.

Pitch number three was like a Burger Clown hamburger: exactly like all the others, right down to the bad taste it left in your mouth.

"WHOOSH!" went the ball.

"YOWCH!" cried Hanky Burns.

"YOU'RE OUT!" yelled the ump.

Ducks trudged back to the dugout, and Stump took his place in the box. Up on the mound, Flicker rolled his trademark toothpick from one side of his mouth to the other. It was his way of laughing, something he always did after whiffing a batter.

"Give it a ride, Stump!" I called from the on-deck circle.

Easier said than done.

Flicker gassed Stump on three straight blur balls.

Then it was my turn.

I rubbed Billy's head for luck, then strode up to the plate and tapped it with my trusty Louisville Slugger.

"Walloper," rasped Flicker in his rattlesnake voice, the old toothpick rolling.

"Flicker." I nodded. Hard to believe we had once been teammates in the All-Star Game. At the moment I felt anything but matey toward him.

"Prepare to meet your doom!"

I didn't say anything. I just cocked my bat.

The first pitch streaked by like a lightning bolt.

"STEE-RIKE ONE!" honked the ump.

The second one slipped past me before I knew it was coming.

"STEE-RIKE TWO!"

The third one I collared like a thief in the night.

"Not so fast!" I said.

The ball didn't say anything. It just whistled like a bottle rocket as it soared into left field and put a dent in the wall. I chugged to second with our first hit of the game.

Flicker didn't like that. He didn't like it so much that he buzzed a heater over Tugboat's head. Our catcher flung his bat and hit the dirt. The ump glared out at the mound.

"None of that," he warned.

"What?" asked Flicker. "It slipped."

Tugboat dusted himself off and managed to lay wood on the next pitch, but not enough to drive it through the infield. The shortstop scooped it on one hop and gunned to first for the out.

The inning ended with Hog City leading 2–0.

As the second frame got under way, I saw my parents hurry into the bleachers. It was the only good thing I saw the whole inning. The Haymakers tacked on two more runs, and we hung another goose egg on the scoreboard.

In the third, Gilly started to tire. The Haymakers touched him for a run on three hits before Skip Lou called for a pitching change. With two outs, two on, and Hoot Fewster flexing his muscles in the batter's box, Gasser took over on the mound and Kid Rabbit came off the bench to replace him at first.

"Good job, Gilly!" I called from third. "You kept us close."

"The only thing close around here is the outfield wall," sneered Hoot. "Watch me blast one over it!"

He never got the chance. Before delivering a single pitch, Gasser caught the runner napping at first and picked him off cleanly.

We went to the bottom of the third trailing by five.

Kid Rabbit led off for us and beat out a worm burner for a single. On the bench, we leaped and hollered and generally carried on as though dollar bills were falling from heaven. Real dollar bills would have been nice. We could have used them to buy a few more hits.

As it turned out, we didn't need to. Stump

followed with a scratch single. Suddenly we had two men on with no outs. The fans started to buzz.

Flicker Pringle didn't like that. He didn't like it one bit. He's a natural grinch, and grinches hate it when other people are happy. So he did what grinches always do. He tried to kill their joy.

First he got Ducks to hit into a double play.

Kid Rabbit scampered down to third, and I came up to bat.

"You again," rasped Flicker, narrowing his eyes.

"Just pitch," I said.

Then he blazed a comet my way.

I don't particularly like grinches, so I tapped it up the middle for a single. Kid Rabbit raced home with our first run. Flicker kicked the mound like it was the dirt's fault. When the dirt could take no more, he whiffed Tugboat.

In the fourth, the Haymakers got the run back on a walk and a triple by Hanky Burns.

We scored again in our half on back-to-back doubles by Velcro and Ocho.

Into the fifth we went, down by four and running out of time. The crowd was hushed and tense as Gasser took the mound. It was so quiet you could practically hear the grass grow. Everybody knew that mounting a comeback against the Haymakers was about as easy as scaling Mount Everest. Barefoot. In a snowstorm. Balancing a beach ball on your nose.

Flicker made things even harder by whacking his second tater of the game. As he trotted around the bases, he veered out of his way to stomp on our toes.

"Watch where you're going, you big lummox!" yelled Gabby from the press box.

I smiled. It was good to know she still had our backs.

"Let's go, guys," I shouted. "Let's play some defense."

The crowd picked up the word and began

to chant: "DEE-FENSE! DEE-FENSE! DEE-FENSE!"

Maybe it was the fans' passion that turned things around. Maybe we just weren't ready to throw in the towel without a fight. Whatever the reason, we flashed some serious leather. First Stump made a diving catch at short. Then Velcro climbed the wall in center to steal a homer. Finally the Glove backhanded a vicious chopper and fired to first from his knees for out number three.

Our sharp play carried over to the bottom half of the inning. Ducks and Stump both ripped hits. Flicker was so mad, he hit me with a pitch. Fortunately it was only a changeup and couldn't have been traveling much faster than a bullet train. I shook it off and trotted down to first.

Tugboat came up with the bases loaded. He took three good cracks, but the ball was like smoke. He swung right through it.

"YOU'RE OUT!" roared the ump, stating the obvious.

Gasser had better luck. He squared to bunt, and Flicker's steamer smacked his bat so hard that the ball ricocheted all the way into right field. Ducks and Stump sprinted in to score.

The lead was down to three.

Velcro cut it to two with a double that brought me home. Ocho followed with a pop-up, our second out of the inning. The Glove stepped in with runners on second and third and Flicker stamping the mound like an enraged bull.

*WHOOSH!* went the ball.

*"YOWCH!"* yelped the catcher.

"STEE-RIKE ONE!" bleated the ump.

*WHOOSH!* went the ball again.

*"YOWCH!"* repeated the catcher.

"STEE-RIKE TWO!" said the ump.

Glove called time and adjusted his wristbands. Fans seized the opportunity to turn their hats inside out and wear them as rally caps. Glove stepped back into the batter's box. Flicker kicked and delivered. The ball sped home, trailing vapor like a jet plane. Glove swung. A crack of thunder shook the park to its foundations. I looked to the sky. I didn't see any clouds. What I saw was the baseball shooting through the air like a comet. Glove had connected!

I don't know where the ball landed. Maybe it never did. But I do know it cleared the wall. With a single mighty clout, Glove had catapulted us into the lead. When the inning ended one batter later, on a final Flicker Pringle strikeout, the Rounders led by a score of 8–7.

We ran onto the diamond three outs away from winning the championship. The crowd roared and stamped its feet, ready to explode.

When the first Haymaker batter rapped a sharp single, things hushed down a little. The second guy drew a walk, and things got quieter still. The third reached on an error, and the fans fell deathly silent.

Ducks brought them back to life with a spectacular diving catch in short left field. His great play saved at least one run from scoring, but it didn't mask the obvious. Gasser was spent. As if to prove the point, the next Haymaker batter clobbered a towering shot to center. The crowd gasped and didn't start breathing again until Ocho chased it down and fired the ball back in before the runner on third had a chance to tag up.

With the tying run stewing at third and Flicker Pringle coming up to bat, Skip Lou had seen enough. He called time and strolled out to the mound. I trotted over to join the confab.

"Great job," he told Gasser. "What do you say we bring in a fresh arm to finish this thing?"

Gasser mopped sweat from his forehead and nodded. "My tank is dry," he admitted.

"You were awesome," I said.

He left the field to a standing ovation.

Skip Lou peered into the dugout.

"Slingshot," he called. "Your time has come."

Slingshot did a double take. He pointed a finger at his chest.

Skip nodded calmly. "Our secret weapon," he said.

Little did he know.

Slowly Slingshot made his way across the diamond. When he reached the mound, Skip handed him the ball. Slingshot took it like it was a hand grenade.

"You've been our best pitcher all year," Skip said. "Heck, you've been our best pitcher for longer than that. There's no one else in the world I'd want out here in this situation."

He jogged back to the bench.

Slingshot gulped. He blinked at the sky. A small gray cloud drifted in front of the sun.

"Forget the weather," I said. "A few clouds are nothing. Leading us out of that cave? That was something. You'll get this guy."

I returned to my position, my fingers firmly crossed the whole way there.

"PLAY BALL!" commanded the ump.

Flicker Pringle twitched his bat like a tiger's tail.

"Welcome back, Rainmaker!" he sneered.

Tugboat flashed a signal. Fastball. Slingshot wound up and delivered.

226

"BALL!" bleated the ump.

The sky darkened ominously.

Slingshot tugged at his cap. He fired another pitch. The crowd held its breath. I did too.

"BALL TWO!"

I felt a raindrop on my face.

"Was that a forkball?" guffawed Flicker. "Please! The only fork you need is one to stick in yourself, because, kid, you are cooked!"

Slingshot tried again.

"BALL THREE!"

Lightning sizzled overhead.

One more missed pitch, and Slingshot would walk in the tying run. It was now or never.

I turned and scanned the crowd, searching for a familiar face. When I spotted it, I nodded.

Joe Wood nodded back.

As the clouds thickened and Slingshot started his windup, the guide leaped to his feet and dashed into the aisle. He raised a forked stick over his head, pointing its prongs straight at the sky. Over in press row, Gabby jumped up and did the same.

Slingshot released the ball. The rain held.

"STEE-RIKE ONE!" called the ump.

Flicker scowled. The crowd roared.

Joe waved his wand in the air. Throughout the park, dozens of fans rose and followed his lead.

Slingshot tossed another pitch.

"STEE-RIKE TWO!"

If the full count bothered Flicker, he didn't let on.

"Rainmaker," he sneered, "I'm going to put you out of your misery. I'm going to hit this pitch into next week."

"It's not going to rain," I shouted as the entire crowd took to its feet. Many fans waved forked branches at the sky. Willow, I trusted. They're said to work best. The rest spread their arms and raised them high. They looked like a bunch of human letter Y's.

Glowering darkly, Flicker Pringle cocked his bat. Slingshot wound up and hummed home a pitch with his whole heart and soul. The instant the ball spun off his fingertips, the sun burst through the gloom and bathed the ballpark in golden light.

The runners broke.

Flicker swung.

"STEE-RIKE THREE!" grunted the ump. "YOU'RE OUT!"

Tugboat raced to the mound and wrapped Slingshot in a bear hug. Sprinting in from our positions, we hoisted the pitcher on our shoulders. Mr. Bones sprang into his arms and licked his face. The Rambletown Rounders had won the game.

The crowd spilled onto the field and joined a conga line led by Joe Wood and Gabby. We latched on to the tail and rode it around the bases. As the head of the line reached home plate and doubled back toward us, Slingshot called to Joe over the frenzied hubbub.

"What in the world were you guys doing out there?" the pitcher hollered.

"Dowsing in reverse," yelled our friend. He winked. "Works every time."

*Give me a forked stick over a forkball any day of the week,* I thought to myself. *And give me a big-hearted pitcher and loyal friends over either of them.*

Then I quit thinking and got back to deliriously bouncing Slingshot in the air. He had done it. He had beaten the rain and the Haymakers. On the arm of Slingshot Slocum we were going out as champs.

# THE RAMBLETOWN ROUNDERS
## FINAL SEASON STATS

Team Manager: Skipper Lou "Skip-to-My-Lou" Clementine

| PLAYER | AVG | HR | RBI | RUNS SCORED |
|---|---|---|---|---|
| The Great Walloper, aka Banjo H. Bishbash, 3B | .562 | 27 | 61 | 35 |
| Ducks Bunion, LF | .306 | 4 | 18 | 30 |
| Octavio "Ocho" James, RF | .288 | 3 | 22 | 22 |
| Gasser Phipps, CF | .313 | 4 | 14 | 21 |
| Stump Plumwhiff, SS | .281 | 5 | 21 | 27 |
| Orlando "Velcro" Ramirez, CF | .402 | 8 | 25 | 32 |
| Ellis "the Glove" Rodgriguez, 2B | .324 | 0 | 11 | 20 |
| Slingshot Slocum, P | .335 | 2 | 20 | 18 |
| Tugboat Tooley, C | .277 | 5 | 16 | 17 |
| Kid Rabbit Winkle, 3B, SS | .299 | 1 | 9 | 11 |
| Gilly Wishes, 1B | .309 | 9 | 31 | 19 |

GRAND SLAM

## Slingshot Slocum
Rambletown Rounders

Pitcher